# ENDINGS AND BEGINNNINGS

WRAK-AYYA: THE AGE OF SHADOWS
BOOK TEN

LEIGH ROBERTS

# CONTENTS

Chapter 1     1
Chapter 2     27
Chapter 3     57
Chapter 4     91
Chapter 5     111
Chapter 6     131
Chapter 7     173
Chapter 8     193
Chapter 9     227
Chapter 10     265
Chapter 11     277
Chapter 12     331

*Please Read*     341
*Acknowledgments*     343

Editing by Joy Sephton  http://www.justemagine.biz
Cover design by Cherie Fox  http://www.cheriefox.com

Sexual activities or events in this book are intended for adults.

ISBN: 978-1-951528-14-0 (ebook)
IBSN: 978-1-951528-27-0 (paperback)

## DEDICATION

*To those who step down halls of wonder, dreaming of answers to the question—*

*What If?*

# CHAPTER 1

Adia tucked her silver-haired offspring close to her and turned her attention back to the crowd. The room started to fill with conversation, heads turning left and right as people speculated on the meaning of Haan's announcement.

Acaraho took a step forward and said loud enough to be heard over the din, "Please everyone; I understand you have a thousand questions, as we do." Then he turned to address Haan, "Adik'Tar, would you elaborate on what you just said?"

"The coming of An'Kru'Tor was foretold centuries ago by the last of the Mothoc Guardians, Pan," Haan said. "It is said that when the Seventh of the Six comes, the Promised One, he will open the path to Wrak-Ashwea, the Age of Light. The Age of Light represents the last hope for Etera. When we opened Kthama Minor, twelve Guardians were created. Six are males. I believe these are the six mentioned in the prediction."

Acaraho thanked the huge Sarnonn, who then bent down to get a closer look at An'Kru. Adia pulled the soft wrap back so Haan could see the offspring more clearly. For a moment, he peered down at An'Kru, taking in the pale skin, the surprising thick silver-white hair-covering. He stared into An'Kru's silver-grey eyes, eyes that stared back with more presence than any newborn should possess. Haan bumped his fist over his heart, bowed slightly, and slowly turned to rejoin his followers.

"This has been a tumultuous morning for all of us. Let us adjourn and go about the day's business," said the new Leader of the High Rocks. "Khon'Tor and Tehya will be here for a few more days, making final arrangements for their move to the Far High Hills. Again, Adia and I wish them great blessings in the new chapter in their lives, as I know you also do."

❧

Khon'Tor stood watching from the back of the Great Chamber, Tehya close at his side. As the crowd started to disperse, one after another came up to say their farewells. Many of the females had tears brewing or were crying outright. Most offered hugs to Tehya. The offspring approached with wide eyes or stood a way off staring at Khon'Tor as if to memorize the moment—their last chance to see the legendary Leader. Males filed up to offer thanks and wish them well. Many of them shared stories they remembered of Khon'Tor or his father.

From the front of the room, Urilla Wuti watched solemnly. A chapter in their history was closing. She hardened her boundaries, overcome by the slurry of emotions welling through the chamber. Off to the side, she watched Akule and Kayah circumvent the line waiting to talk to Khon'Tor and Tehya and sneak down the tunnel leading to their quarters. Urilla then watched as the other High Council members approached Acaraho and Adia, and as Harak'Sar waited for a turn to speak with Khon'Tor and Tehya.

Recognizing Harak'Sar's station, others allowed him to step in out of turn. "I realize it will take a few days, as Acaraho said, for you to go through your belongings and decide what to take. I will wait to journey back with you if you do not mind. In the meantime, I am arranging for better quarters for you at the Far High Hills." He turned to Tehya, a slight smile crossing his face, "More spacious. Closer to your parents, but not *too* close."

Whatever Harak'Sar had just said, Urilla Wuti could feel it had released a great deal of Khon'Tor's tension. She got up and went over to them.

"We are talking about plans for the trip back to the Far High Hills," Harak'Sar explained to Urilla Wuti as she joined the circle.

She smiled. "I will return with you when you leave."

"Of course," Harak'Sar said. "It will be good to have you back home. I know Iella will be very happy to have your company again." Then he stepped aside to let the rest of the well-wishers have their moment with the former Leader of the High Rocks.

It took some time for the chamber to empty, with the People saying their goodbyes to Khon'Tor and Tehya, congratulating Acaraho and Adia, and wanting a peek at An'Kru.

Finally, no one was left waiting to speak to them, and Khon'Tor and Tehya were alone.

"It has been a draining morning. Would you like to rest before we start packing?" Khon'Tor asked her.

"No. If you do not mind, I would rather get to it. The longer we stay here, the longer the heartache will last," she answered.

Khon'Tor frowned and put his arm around his mate's tiny waist. "Please do not feel bad about leaving the High Rocks. I will find my place somehow."

Tehya took his hand, and they left for the Leader's Quarters.

It was a long time since they had last been there together. Tehya immediately started moving about the room, picking up one thing after another and making a pile on the softsit.

"I do not suppose we can take this with us." She turned and smiled impishly as she looked down at the vast creation Oh'Dar had made for them.

"No, probably not," he answered, a brief smile crossing his lips.

"I hope Acaraho and Adia enjoy it as much as we have," she said, plopping down on it, grinning more widely and giving him a wink.

Khon'Tor could not help but break out in a wide grin.

"I appreciate your trying to keep this light-hearted, just as I appreciated Harak'Sar's humorous comment about our new living space not being located too close to your parents. Perhaps some of his harshness toward me has lightened a bit, though I do not know why."

"I do not condone in any way what you did, Adoeete," Tehya said, sitting upright, "as I know you would not want me to. But humility loosens the set jaw of judgment. Perhaps he has come to realize that none of us is perfect."

Then she changed the subject. "Can I take the fluorite?" she asked, glancing over at the beautiful purplish stones charging in the rays of sunlight that shone down through the overhead ventilation shafts.

"Of course. Any of it. All of it. I do not see us coming back often. Please be thorough. Do not leave behind anything you want."

Tehya continued around the room and dragged Kweeu's bed over to the *going* corner. She stooped over and picked up her wraps that were habitually scattered about, then went through her personal items in the private area. Lastly, she gathered up Arismae's toys, her extra blankets, everything they had not taken when they last vacated Kthama.

"What are you taking?" she stopped to ask him, feeling him watching her every move.

"Memories," he said.

Tehya dropped Arismae's belongings on the pile and came over to put her arms around him. She tilted her head back to look up at his face.

"Yes. And we have many more to make, you and I, and Arismae."

Khon'Tor pulled her closer into his arms. She happily rested her head against his hard barrel chest, and he kissed her hair.

"We must not forget the Keeping Stones," she lifted her head to say. "And our personal care items. Oh dear, some of these things will have to wait until it is actually time to leave because we will need them for a few more days."

"Collect what you can. Acaraho will provide packing baskets," he said. "It is fine to gather it all in one spot for now, even though we will not be leaving for a few days; there are still many more people wishing to say goodbye to you and Arismae."

"And you, Adoeete," she added.

Back in the Great Chamber, Harak'Sar, Risik'Tar, and Lesharo'Mok stood talking with Acaraho and Adia.

"Before we leave the High Rocks, perhaps we should call a High Council meeting," said Harak'Sar. Both he and Risik'Tar were fighting their inclination to stare at the silver-colored offspring in Adia's arms.

"I agree, but not today," said Acaraho. "Adia needs to tend to An'Kru, and this has been a tiring morning. Tomorrow."

"That is fine," said Harak'Sar, as Risik'Tar and Lesharo'Mok nodded in agreement.

"After first meal, then. I will make sure the usual room is available," said Acaraho.

"By the way," Risik'Tar said to him, "Khon'Tor is not invited."

"I would not expect so, as he is no longer our Leader," Acaraho replied.

"I just felt it needed to be pointed out," Risik'Tar said.

Acaraho nodded. "Till tomorrow then." He then placed his hand on the small of Adia's back and led her away.

Once they were out of earshot, Harak'Sar turned to Risik'Tar, "Was that necessary? Why would you say that? You underestimate Acaraho if you think he would have invited Khon'Tor."

"Yes, you are correct; I did not need to say it."

"He embodies the highest ethics," said

Lesharo'Mok. "Even though Khon'Tor raped Adia, Acaraho has been more than fair and his actions and judgments above reproach."

The rest of the day progressed slowly.

"That was harder than I thought it would be," said Acaraho. "For one thing, we certainly were not expecting that announcement from Haan."

"In a way, I am relieved. It is as if more of the pieces are falling together," Adia said.

"An'Kru is going to draw a lot of attention. But perhaps in time, the novelty will wear off. It did with Oh'Dar," said her mate.

"At any rate, I felt that everyone accepted him," she continued. "There is so much to talk about; my head is spinning. I saw Akule and Kayah leave the room early. Perhaps knowing Khon'Tor is leaving the High Rocks will give her some peace of mind. Though I did not get a feeling of relief from her, which troubles me."

"It is an unfortunate turn of events," said Acaraho. "Akule and Kayah had asked to move to the Far High Hills. Now that Khon'Tor and Tehya are moving there, it seems they have little choice but to stay here."

"That explains why I felt no sense of relief from her when Khon'Tor announced they were leaving

Kthama, and it explains why they left the Great Chamber so expeditiously," she said.

After a moment, she continued, "And Risik'Tar. Why would he think you might invite Khon'Tor to the High Council meeting?"

"I have no idea—unless he thinks any loyalty I have to Khon'Tor would overshadow my better judgment." Acaraho sighed. "Get some rest. I am afraid it will be a while before things feel normal again."

After taking care of An'Kru, they settled down together, and though the full darkness of night had not yet descended, they immediately fell asleep.

The next morning came soon enough. The end of first meal found Acaraho standing in the meeting room before Harak'Sar, Lesharo'Mok, Risik'Tar, Urilla Wuti, and Adia. Mapiya was taking care of An'Kru for a little while, leaving Adia to give her full attention to the present goings-on.

"It is time to do as we said, that once the matter of the leadership of the High Rocks was settled, we would again have the Healers and Helpers attend the High Council meetings."

"I agree," said Lesharo'Mok. "We need the checks and balances that the females' insight will bring."

"I also agree," Risik'Tar answered, eyeing Acaraho carefully. "We discussed it at the Far High Hills."

"Decided then. The next order of business is one I have already discussed with Adia. Due to the peculiar circumstances, she is now both Second and Third Rank. To create the balance that having a Second and Third rank was designed to provide, I submit that the new High Protector of the People of the High Rocks should join us as Kthama's Second Rank."

The other Leaders exchanged glances. "That seems a logical substitution," Harak'Sar commented.

"Then First Guard Awan will be joining us at future meetings," Acaraho replied. "Also, it has been decades since there was a full High Council meeting —one that includes all the Brothers' Chiefs from the tribes associated with each of our communities."

"We also have the issue of not having an Overseer, lest we forget," Lesharo'Mok reminded them.

"Before we get into that, I have a proposal of a serious nature to put forward," said Harak'Sar.

Acaraho relinquished the floor and sat next to Adia as the Leader of the Far High Hills stood up. "This is no doubt a sensitive issue. Please hear me out before you decide against the idea."

Khon'Tor had finished the morning meal and was winding his way back through Kthama to join Tehya in their quarters. On the way, he passed by the meeting room and heard the familiar voices. *They are*

*having a High Council meeting. Another door in my life*
*closed. Who am I to be now?*

Suddenly wistful, Khon'Tor turned back the way
he had come and left Kthama. He wandered with no
real destination. Nearly every path, every turn, held a
memory of some kind. Before long, he was standing
at the beginning of the path that had led to the Healer's Cove but was now the entrance to Kthama Minor.
The same path on which, decades ago, he had
assaulted and raped Adia.

He stood a while, lost in thought, then retraced
his steps and continued on. The winding path where
his father, Ranax'Tor, had taught him how to run
swiftly without losing his footing. He passed the oak
trees he had climbed as a youth, and the best grove
for picking the fall fruit. There were many other
places where memories lived of his father instructing
him; he remembered learning to feel the magnetic
currents, which stretched across Etera like a web.
Here were the soft riverbanks where he had played
under his mother's watchful eye; there was the valley
where he had uprooted trees after Hakani's torments.
He passed the steep area where he had worked off
frustration and built his strength, and the grassy spot
where he had spent lonesome nights out under the
stars. Still fresh in his mind was the memory of the
shooting star the night of Chief Ogima's death.

When he came across the alcove where he had
raped his unknown victim, the one whom no one
could identify, he stopped a moment and said a

prayer for her. Memories of her face sometimes haunted him at night, when he would lie there wondering what had become of her.

Khon'Tor's steps took him down the paths surrounding Kthama to the valley where he, Acaraho, and Awan had faced what they believed were to be their final moments. Just as the path to Kthama Minor bloomed profusely with new life, so did this valley and the path the Sarnonn Guardians had taken to reach it. The discarded spears of the rebel Sarnonn forces, dropped after Staf'Tor had appeared, were already almost entirely hidden, intertwined with the thick growth.

Finally, he walked up the path that wound high above the Great River to where Hakani had first tried to kill herself and Nootau and had subsequently succeeded in taking her own life. Nootau, the son he could never claim. So many life-changing events had taken place here. This was where Tehya had delivered Arismae and where Oh'Dar had miraculously saved the newborn when she stopped breathing.

Khon'Tor walked over to the very edge of the path and looked across to the cascade of waters falling down into the Great River below. The rich, humid smell of the water rose up to greet him—a light mist providing some relief from the heat of the day.

He stood in the same spot where he had beseeched the Great Spirit for forgiveness, where he had pressed the Waschini blade against his neck, ready to settle the debt he owed for his crimes. It was ironic that in the end, Hakani's words, the words of the one with whom he had shared such a tormented relationship, had shifted him from the intention of taking his own life.

After a moment of silence, as he was turning to leave, Khon'Tor let his gaze once again sweep the area. A glint of sunlight caught his attention, reflecting off something in the weeds. He stooped down and swept the high grasses back and forth with his hand, finally finding the cause. The Waschini knife Oh'Dar had given him, a gift brought back from the last trip to Shadow Ridge.

Khon'Tor pulled it loose from the tangled growth. He wiped the blade on the grass, removing the accumulated dirt.

A shiny black crow landed on a thick branch of a nearby tree and tilted its head back and forth, eyeing Khon'Tor, before launching off and flying away with a loud cry.

*Everywhere I look has a memory, but it seems that now the painful ones overshadow the happy ones. Perhaps it is best that my days here are over. As for forgiving myself, I do not know where the secret lies, but I believe I will never find peace here.*

He took a last look around and slowly returned to Kthama, the Waschini blade in his hand.

Back in the secluded meeting room, now the place where the High Council always assembled when at Kthama, Harak'Sar continued. "As Adik'Tar Acaraho has just pointed out, we all need the insights and viewpoints that the Healers and Helpers can bring. In these tumultuous times, we need, more than ever, all the life experience and wisdom we can garner." He paced the room as Khon'Tor had done so many times, and all eyes followed him.

"We have just lost a very valuable member of our High Council. One whose leadership has brought us through trial after trial. One who has committed serious crimes, but the value of whose experience, I put to you, is important to the High Council and should not be permitted to diminish."

Everyone exchanged glances.

Risik'Tar spoke up, "You are talking of Khon'Tor?"

"Yes, I am."

"After what he did? How can you even suggest it? He was removed from the leadership in shame," Risik'Tar barked.

"He was removed from the leadership by Kurak'Kahn, who, lest you forget, has committed serious crimes of his own." Harak'Sar frowned at Risik'Tar. "And his motives in doing so are suspect." He turned back to the group and recounted Kurak'Kahn's accusation that Khon'Tor was responsible for his niece's death.

When Harak'Sar was done, Acaraho stood to

speak, "It is true. Kurak'Kahn came prepared to murder Khon'Tor, using a jhorallax, a weapon banned long ago for being too brutal and cruel. He counted on inflamed emotions to rush us into judgment against Khon'Tor. He intended for Khon'Tor to die, in which case there would most likely have been no need to clean his wounds, and the spikes embedded deep in his flesh would have gone unnoticed."

"The fact of Kurak'Kahn's guilt does not pardon Khon'Tor's action," said Risik'Tar.

"No one is proposing that," said Harak'Sar. "But you cannot overlook the decades of wisdom and insight Khon'Tor brought us."

"What role are you proposing he play?" asked Lesharo'Mok. "You are the Leader of the Far High Hills. He has no position of authority there. You have both a High Protector and a First Guard. Unless you are thinking of creating something—"

"I have heard mention here of a Circle of Counsel," answered Harak'Sar. "Within our communities, we also all have those whom we turn to for advice. I believe it would be wise for each Leader to officially create and proclaim his own Circle of Counsel. To that end, Khon'Tor would serve as one of my high advisors within my own circle," Harak'Sar explained.

"We are arguing about justice versus mercy," said Risik'Tar.

"Are you proposing that justice has not been served on Khon'Tor?" asked Harak'Sar. "We agreed to let the victim determine the punishment. Kayah herself declared Kah-Sol'Rin. Are you proposing perpetual retaliation by holding his crime against him forever?"

"I cannot believe you are bringing this up now," said Risik'Tar. "We have not even discussed the Chamber of the Ancients, a burial tomb proving the existence of ancestors that until a short while ago, we did not even know we had. We are still recovering from one shock after another," he added. "It is not the time for this!"

"It is true," interjected Lesharo'Mok. "We have not discussed what we saw. But Harak'Sar has put the subject to us, so let us deal with it. I want to hear from Adia." Turning to his niece, he said, "You have suffered at Khon'Tor's hands. What say you of this?"

Adia slowly stood and walked to the front to address the group.

"Through the years, I have grappled with the concept of forgiveness. It is no doubt easier to forgive the person who wronged you when they have realized they were wrong and express regret. As did Khon'Tor. None of us can dispute that he has changed. The passing years have proven this change to be genuine. In my heart, I see no threat in Khon'Tor to any female. And Harak'Sar is right; consider his leadership that has guided us through the years. Most recently, there has been his foresight in asking Oh'Dar to start instructing us and our offspring in the Waschini language. Before that was his decision to give Kthama Minor to Haan's people, who are now our staunch allies. The question we are trying to answer is, regardless of redemption, once punishment has been delivered, should we continue to hold the deeds against the perpetrator?"

Risik'Tar addressed Adia, "How can you say that what he did should be dismissed? You, of all people, should know what it is like to suffer from his cruelty. If the stories are true, he made your life very difficult after you brought the Waschini offspring to the High Rocks."

"As far as his behavior toward me after I rescued Oh'Dar is concerned, yes. He set out to make it as difficult for me as possible. But again, he is not the same person who committed those earlier acts—" and her voice faded.

"Well then," Risik'Tar snapped, "what of Kurak'Kahn's niece? As he pointed out, she is not here to speak for herself."

"Everything Kurak'Kahn told us is hearsay," said Harak'Sar. "We have no way of knowing if what he claimed is true. It is equally possible that her mate, Berak, threw her from the cliff, or that she did kill herself but was driven more by his treatment of her than by Khon'Tor's alleged rape. If he did assault her, she lived with it for some time. And since she is not here to pass judgment, are we, the High Council, now changing our earlier agreement that the victims should decide what price would be extracted for the crime committed against them?"

As Urilla Wuti slowly stood to speak, all eyes turned in her direction. "We have been witness to Khon'Tor's exemplary leadership of Kthama and his contributions to the welfare of all the People. May I remind you, as Harak'Sar has already pointed out, that this very council determined that the victims would set the punishment, which would be the total of the judgment against Khon'Tor. The first victim ordered fifty lashes but declared it completed at fifteen. The second victim wanted no punishment exacted, having found peace with what he did to her and having moved on. We have no way of knowing what Kurak'Kahn's niece would have wanted—if Khon'Tor indeed assaulted her. There have been no crimes that I can remember of this magnitude among our people; we have never before had to wrestle with situations like this."

She looked from one to the other, "We will not solve this today. We must decide it after emotions have settled. Risik'Tar is right; we have been through too much lately with no time for any reflection and recovery. Please collect yourselves. Then I urge you all to search your hearts and decide what your position on this will be. It is not up to us whether Harak'Sar avails himself of Khon'Tor's wisdom and experience at the Far High Hills. That is not our decision. But the question we must answer is, once punishment has been declared and delivered, should the person be allowed to continue with his or her life and try to find whatever happiness or purpose they can? Or is there an ongoing price to be exacted for their crimes?"

Everyone slowly nodded agreement, even Risik'-Tar. Acaraho had already said what he thought and now kept his silence, though he had taken in every word, every nuance, as the others spoke.

After a moment, he stood to address the others. "Before we leave, there is another matter to resolve. And I believe it can be resolved fairly quickly. We have no Overseer. Until we can convene a meeting that includes the Leaders from the Little River, the Great Pines, and the High Red Rocks, we need to appoint someone in a temporary capacity."

All heads slowly turned to Urilla Wuti, then back to Acaraho.

"I am honored by your belief in me," the Healer said. "I would be willing to serve until all the Leaders can attend another High Council meeting."

"I can think of no one more suited to be Overseer than you," replied Harak'Sar. "I am confident the other Leaders when they arrive, will concur with our recommendation, even though they have not lived through the recent events we have. The truth is, the communities of the Little River, the Great Pines, and the High Red Rocks are never as involved because of the distances separating us."

Acaraho called for those there to stand if they agreed to appoint Urilla Wuti as the temporary Overseer.

"It is agreed then," he said. "By unanimous

consent of the members here, Urilla Wuti will serve as the new Overseer of the People's High Council until such time as she is permanently awarded the position, or another is selected."

Later that afternoon, Urilla Wuti joined Harak'Sar, Acaraho, Adia, and Nootau in the eating area. Nootau was holding An'Kru, who was wrapped snugly in a soft hide blanket.

Harak'Sar addressed Urilla Wuti, "I will be returning home to the Far High Hills as soon as Khon'Tor and Tehya are ready to leave. Will you be ready soon?"

"Yes, I will be ready," she answered.

Nootau turned to his parents. "I would like to go with them to the Far High Hills. Iella had just started teaching me the different plants and their uses when we had to come home."

Adia cocked her head, "I do not remember you being interested in healing matters, Nootau? What changed?"

"I have always wanted to learn about them, Mama," Nootau admitted. "I just kept quiet because Oh'Dar was interested too. Much here was harder for him than for me. I felt he should have something of his own, so I set my interest aside."

Adia closed her eyes for a moment. "That was very kind of you, Nootau, though I am sorry you gave up something you wanted to learn. So it is not just Iella that calls you to the Far High Hills?"

Nootau chuckled, "It is of little consequence, Mama. I had other interests to pursue, and right now, you are too busy to teach me. As far as Iella is concerned, well, yes, I do really like her, and I would like to spend more time with her and the friends I made while I was there before. I will make sure I am ready to leave."

Adia nodded and looked over at the older Healer. "I am going to miss you so much."

Urilla Wuti smiled, a bit sadly. "And I will miss you. But we both know it is time."

Adia reached out to take An'Kru from Nootau. She cuddled the newborn close.

Eventually, Nootau, Harak'Sar, and Acaraho rose, leaving the two Healers to each other.

Urilla Wuti turned to Adia. "I do not know if Nootau has Healer ability. You told me of his visit from Pan, in which she gave him An'Kru's name. As you know, usually we can sense Healers early. And yet, I was a Healer's Helper before I was found to be a Healer. It was only then that my grandmother's sister, Sihu Onida, began working with me. So he may also turn out to have Healer abilities."

"Sihu Onida was sister to your mother's mother? I never knew that," exclaimed Adia.

"Yes. She was a great Healer; it was she who mentored me."

Adia fell silent a moment before continuing. "But

if Nootau has Healer abilities—well, it would be unusual for a male."

"I believe it is as E'ranale told us; many abilities are being augmented. Perhaps that includes those who have remained dormant until now," Urilla Wuti suggested.

"Urilla," Adia continued softly. "Do you remember when you first started training me? Before Nootau and Nimida were born. You told me you had a vision of a network of Healers who could communicate through the Connection—that because of the coming challenges, we would need to reach each other across great distances."

"Yes. That was and is still my vision. Though, I think the Connection may not be this conduit."

"Yes. I have had the same thought," said Adia. "Perhaps it is not the Connection. Perhaps we can unite in the Corridor itself."

Urilla Wuti nodded.

"The benefit of the Corridor over the Connection is that there is no merging of consciousness. So individual privacy is not breached," said Adia. "And other than when I tried to rescue Khon'Tor and Tehya, we have never attempted to connect with more than one consciousness. Perhaps the Corridor is the solution, after all."

"I wonder what E'ranale would say about that," smiled the older Healer.

Back at the Far High Hills, Kurak'Kahn's mate had finally arrived. High Protector Thorak greeted her. "He will be delighted to see you, Larara," he said as he led her to her mate's quarters.

"As I will be to see him," she replied

Though the former Overseer was no longer confined under guard to his quarters, he seldom left other than to eat. He trusted that Acaraho had kept his word and not disclosed any crimes, but he imagined judgment in everyone's eyes. *And how am I to tell Larara what I have done? Should I even do so? No matter how long I think about this, I cannot come to a decision. She has weathered so much; can I add this burden to what she is already carrying?*

Thorak stepped aside and motioned for Larara to enter. Kurak'Kahn immediately stood upon seeing his mate, and as the High Protector closed the door, she quickly crossed the room into his welcoming arms.

"I have missed you so," he whispered into her hair, inhaling the sweet fragrance of rose and mint.

"I am sorry I could not come here sooner. There is so much sadness back home. Linoi's parents are grieving deeply. I knew you needed me here, but—" She stopped.

"I understand. I had expected to be here longer, or I would not have sent for you. But now, I am ready to leave as soon as you are able. Perhaps tomorrow morning?"

"Yes, of course. But tell me, what new burden is

weighing on you so heavily? I can see it in your face. And I am sorry to see how tired you look," she said gently.

*I have never lied to her. In all these years, am I to start now?*

"These past few months have worn me down, as you know better than anyone. I have seen things, heard things that have shaken the foundation of what I believed to be true. I need time to process it all. But I do have some good news. The Leaders of the other communities have offered to help with the search for U'Kail. They know we do not have the numbers to sustain a wide and robust search. It is a long shot, but I know you have not given up hope of finding him."

"I know there is little chance he is alive, but any hope is better than none. Oh, if they could find him, we would at least have something of her here with us. At the next High Council meeting, please be sure to convey my gratitude for their offer of help."

"I must tell you; I am no longer Overseer."

Larara searched his face before confessing, "Good. I am glad; you have done enough. Let someone else carry the burden I have seen you struggle with through the years. I am proud of you for stepping down. Perhaps when we are settled, you can tell me what has disturbed you so."

Kurak'Kahn could not bring himself to tell her the truth. Instead, he retrieved a small pouch from his personal things. He handed it to his mate. "Here,

I asked Oh'Dar, the Waschini adopted by the Healer Adia, to make this. I hope it pleases you."

Larara took the soft bundle and opened it carefully. She gasped when she saw the row of beautiful stones. She held it up and let it twist and sparkle in front of them both. "It is beautiful. Oh, thank you so much for your kindness. And I must thank Oh'Dar if ever I see him again.

Kurak'Kahn smiled at seeing his mate's pleasure but was not sure she knew what it really was. "Come here," he said. He took the necklace and stepped behind her. He placed it around her neck and fastened it, letting it drape onto her chest.

"Oooh," she exclaimed, looking down, touching it, and running her fingers lightly over the stones.

"Now," said Kurak'Kahn, "Let us go to the evening meal, and then we will retire. I long to lie next to you again. We can leave for home at first light." He took her hand and led her out and down the hall to the eating area.

The next morning, Thorak sent a messenger to the High Rocks to tell Harak'Sar that Kurak'Kahn and his mate had left the Far High Hills.

## CHAPTER 2

Their last day at Kthama dawned. The day before had been hectic with Tehya saying goodbye to her friends, and they were both exhausted by bedtime. However, both awoke early after a restless night. Though she had not been disturbed by the recurring nightmare about Akar'-Tor, Tehya had still slept fitfully. Her every movement had woken Khon'Tor, who was expecting her to wake, screaming, as she had in the past.

While Tehya nursed Arismae, Khon'Tor packed their belongings into the baskets Acaraho had arranged to be delivered.

Finally, it was time. Tehya met the guards at the door and showed them what was going. The males picked up the baskets and stepped outside. Tehya followed with Arismae and Kweeuu and waited in the hallway for her mate.

Khon'Tor took one last look around. The

sleeping mat where they had shared their first love-mating—what he had feared at the time would be their last. The morning rays now streaming down from the overhead shafts that while he watched her sleep, always softly lit Tehya's hair splayed over the pillow. The work counter where they laughed together as she prepared their meals, or simply sat, talking. The softsit Oh'Dar had made for them and the excellent use they had put it to.

Finally, his gaze fell on the empty corner where the Leader's Staff had stood for decades. He remembered the moment it had passed from his father's grasp to his own. The excitement and fear he felt at that moment, even as he grieved his father's passing. He had wanted so much to make his father proud but was so afraid he might not be able to live up to Ranax'Tor's expectations and example. Now, Khon'-Tor's dreams of one day handing the Leader's Staff to his own son—shattered.

The emptiness of the corner became unbearable, just one more reminder of his own failings, and he had to close his eyes to bear the pain. *Forgive me, Father. I am sorry I let you down. If you are united with Mother in the Great Spirit, I also ask her forgiveness. I betrayed the faith you placed in me. I dishonored the House of 'Tor.*

He took one more look at the empty corner, turned, and walked out of the Leader's Quarters for the last time.

Khon'Tor and Tehya traveled toward the lower level of Kthama, where they were to meet Harak'Sar, Nootau, and Urilla Wuti. Along the way, they heard Adia's voice calling out.

"Khon'Tor. Wait, please!" They stopped and turned to see the Healer hurrying after them with Oh'Dar a few paces behind.

"I sent word to the village that you were leaving. Oh'Dar wanted to say farewell," Adia said, giving Oh'Dar time to catch up.

"I almost missed you," he gasped, bent over and trying to catch his breath. He leaned down and petted Kweeuu, who had come over to greet him.

Khon'Tor stood silently looking at the Waschini. His own words came back to him, words he had harshly spoken to Adia years ago. *The presence of this offspring creates a danger to all the People. It is an encumbrance. It is weak and frail and will never be able to function as a contributing member of our community. It will never be allowed to leave, so it will spend the rest of its life here. What will become of it when it reaches pairing age? When it is filled with a male's natural desires? None of the females will have it—so pitiful and repulsive. It will never be a provider or a protector. It will live and die alone, separated from its own kind. That is the life to which you have sentenced it, Adia. That is the life to which you have condemned it. Death would have been a kindness.*

Tehya chuckled and walked over to Oh'Dar, Arismae on her hip, and put a hand on his arm. "Are you alright?" she smiled as he slowly straightened up.

"Yes, thank you," he grinned. "I know I will see you again, but I wanted to wish you well in your new home. I will continue the Waschini language lessons here, just as you asked, Khon'Tor. The young ones are doing really well, you should know. I sometimes hear them practicing with each other, much to their parent's chagrin. I think they like having a secret language," he grinned. "But their advantage will not last long. Even more of the adults will be starting lessons soon, and should you want, at some point, I could come to the Far High Hills as well."

Khon'Tor nodded. "Thank you, Oh'Dar. I hope your father will be supporting this mission to teach Whitespeak and the Waschini writing. The history of the People must be recorded in detail. And I mean the truth of it. As much as you can uncover." Then he added, "Even the failings of those such as me."

Oh'Dar nodded.

Tehya gave Oh'Dar a hug. "I will miss seeing you so often; we have more lessons of our own to continue. Please come and visit. And bring Acise." Then she whispered in his ear, "*I have the gift you gave me. I will keep it safe.*"

"Are you learning Whitespeak?" Khon'Tor asked his mate.

"No. Do you not remember? After I was rescued

from Akar, Oh'Dar offered to teach me some self-defense moves that his father taught him. Since he was so much smaller than his peers, he had to be quicker and a step ahead, and he thought if I knew some ways to defend myself, it might help the nightmares go away." Tehya frowned, disturbed that he had forgotten the conversation.

Khon'Tor shook his head. "I do not remember, but that is good. Anything that helps you feel better, Saraste'. Thank you, Oh'Dar," he added.

Then Khon'Tor stepped forward and put his right hand on Oh'Dar's shoulder in the People's gesture of brotherhood. Oh'Dar, deeply moved by the gesture of acceptance, reached up to return the sign by placing his hand on Khon'Tor's shoulder. The two males nodded at each other.

After a moment, Khon'Tor turned and said to the guards who were standing waiting, "Come. It is time for us to go."

Then, without turning back, Khon'Tor, Tehya with Arismae now in her sling, and Kweeuu moved down toward the tunnel that followed the Mother Stream, toward their new home at the Far High Hills.

Adia turned to her Waschini son. "You have not yet met your little brother."

"I have time before I need to return to the village," Oh'Dar said.

"Pakuna is watching him; come," and Adia led Oh'Dar off to meet little An'Kru. The offspring was sleeping when they arrived at Pakuna's quarters. Adia moved quietly over to where he lay. Because the weather was warm, he was uncovered, and his silver-white hair and pale skin contrasted sharply with the darker hides on which he was resting.

She turned to Oh'Dar before motioning him over. "Before you see him, let me assure you that he is perfectly healthy."

Oh'Dar frowned and quietly approached. He looked into the nest, quickly glanced at his mother, then stared for the longest time at the little offspring who lay there, so vulnerable.

Oh'Dar finally stepped away and his mother followed. "How is this possible?" he asked. "His coloring reminds me of the newly-created Sarnonn Guardians."

"So much has happened since we last spoke— even since you last spoke with Nootau. I know your brother sent you the news that Khon'Tor had stepped down and that your father is now Leader of the High Rocks. But did he also tell you the researchers discovered that your father is of 'Tor descent?" Adia went on to tell Oh'Dar about Haan's announcement at the transfer of leadership cere-mony, the meaning of An'Kru's name, and even the story behind Nootau's knowledge that the offspring should be named An'Kru.

"So he is some type of Guardian?" Oh'Dar asked.

"I believe so. The Guardians only come through the 'Tor line," his mother answered.

"Still. From everything I have learned about attributes passed through bloodlines, this combination should not be possible. Something else must have happened to cause this."

Adia thought back to Kthama Minor's opening. The bright light which had shot up from the vortex below Kthama, called forth by the Sarnonn Ror'Eckrah. The same light that transformed the generator monoliths in the meadow from granite boulders to sparkling crystals. The same force that transformed the six Sarnonn pairs into Guardians. She remembered doubling over, clutching her belly, at the same time the Aezaiterian force had burst forth from the vortex. *Why did I not see this? The connection is so obvious. It was not a natural occurrence —how An'Kru looks is the result of supernatural inter-vention.* Pan's words made even more sense to her now.

"You are right. I need to sit with this a while," Adia told her son.

"I know you must be worried about what awaits him, but we both know that whatever his destiny is, it will be significant to our people."

"Before you go back to the village, please give me a few more minutes." Adia led Oh'Dar out of the room and a little way down the passage. She told him everything she could think of to bring him up to date, other than that which was confidential to the

High Council members. When she was done, she hugged him. "Give my love to Acise and her parents."

"I will not speak to them of this," Oh'Dar said. "This is your story to tell as you wish." And he hugged his mother goodbye.

At the entrance to the Mother Stream, Khon'Tor and Tehya soon met up with Harak'Sar, Nootau, and Urilla Wuti. Acaraho and the new High Protector were waiting there in the cool, dim light with the guards and the packed belongings.

"Is this everything?" Acaraho asked, motioning to the baskets.

"Almost," and Khon'Tor turned to Awan. "You have something of mine, but I cannot take it with me now." He turned back to Acaraho, "With your permission, I would like to return sometime to get it, sooner rather than later."

Acaraho replied, "Of course. You are welcome here. I apologize if in any way that was not made clear."

"Thank you," said Khon'Tor quietly.

Acaraho watched until the travelers had disappeared from view.

Over the next few days, the group traveled mostly in silence, all lost in their own thoughts. The trip was uneventful, and they finally surfaced from the tunnel, blinking against the light, and followed the route to the entrance of the Far High Hills. As they walked, they heard the watchers' calls announcing their arrival. By the time the group reached the entrance, a number of people had gathered to greet them.

Harak'Sar welcomed them all, giving a special, respectful nod to Urilla Wuti.

"I am glad to see you back, Nootau. We kept your room ready in case you decided to pay us a return visit."

He continued, addressing all the travelers, "Please make yourselves at home, and we will talk at evening meal."

A relatively small couple stepped out of the crowd and the male, medium brown in color, approached Khon'Tor and Tehya. It was Reckodd, Tehya's father. It was some time since Reckodd had been in Khon'Tor's presence, and he seemed to be giving his daughter's mate a thorough looking-over.

His mate, Vosha, stood next to him, and Khon'Tor once again noted how much Tehya favored her mother. Vosha was also delicately built, with finer features than most of the People. He said nothing but suddenly wondered if Tehya had shared what she had learned at the Wall of Records of their Waschini heritage.

Vosha nodded to Khon'Tor. "I remember when you came to the Far High Hills, just before the last Ashwea Awhidi. I will admit we were nervous that our daughter was being paired with a legend."

"Legends are not always founded in reality," Khon'Tor replied. "Now that your daughter and I will be living here, we will get to know each other well. And you can decide for yourself where the truth does and does not lie, in the legend of the so-called *great* Khon'Tor," he smiled. "But I will tell you that no one could love your daughter more than I do," and he bowed the slightest bit.

Vosha smiled and turned to embrace her daughter. Tehya handed Arismae to Khon'Tor to hold while they hugged.

"You have new quarters, by the way; did Adik'Tar 'Sar tell you?"

"Yes, Mother; I am anxious to see them."

"Oh, let me have little Arismae, may I?" and Vosha took the offspring from Khon'Tor's arms. Arismae reached out and grasped some of the fringe on Vosha's sheath, then she looked up at her grandmother and smiled.

Harak'Sar signaled for the High Protector to show them to their new quarters.

"All the belongings you left here were moved for you," said Thorak. "I hope you do not mind."

"Thank you," Khon'Tor said, and he and Tehya left with Thorak while Vosha gladly took charge of

Arismae. Several guards carried the baskets for them.

The tunnels, which were so familiar to Tehya, were still unfamiliar to Khon'Tor. He studied the route, not wanting to get lost finding his way around. So hard to let go of Kthama and learn new habits, new protocols. They passed the eating area, where the few gathered stared at them as they moved through.

Finally, they stood in what was to be their new home. Tehya looked around and immediately spotted the white feather and her necklace on a table by the sleeping mat. She then saw the beautiful nest already prepared for Arismae. She fingered the soft blankets and marveled at how comforting and safe it looked. She turned around and smiled profusely at Khon'Tor.

Though still not as big as the Leader's Quarters at Kthama, it was more well-appointed than their temporary room had been, spacious, with an actual separate sleeping area. Two ventilation shafts gave more than enough light to charge her precious fluorite, which gave such a beautiful glow in the night hours.

The food baskets had already been stocked, and fresh water awaited their use. It was obvious someone had taken care that they should feel welcome.

"Thank you. And please thank Harak'Sar for me until I can do it in person. This is a generous provision, and I am very grateful," Khon'Tor said to Thorak.

"The layout of Kayerm is different, but much is fairly similar to Kthama, I am sure. In no time, it will feel like home."

Khon'Tor nodded.

Before Thorak left with his guards, he added, "In case you do not know, Harak'Sar asked me to tell you that Kurak'Kahn and his mate left here several days ago. They have returned to their own community."

Once Thorak was out of the way, Tehya ran across the room and threw herself up into Khon'Tor's arms. She clasped her hands around his neck and pressed her face against his skin, inhaling his familiar male scent.

"I am so glad you are happy," he whispered into her ear as he held her tightly, luxuriating in her softness and familiar scent.

"Oh, Adoeete, I am. But I also know this is not your home," she said, leaning back to look into his eyes. "And for that, my heart is heavy."

"I am happy seeing you happy, Saraste'. Come, take me on a tour while we have time. I am anxious for the day when the tunnels and halls here start to feel familiar."

"Let me first unpack a few things, then we can go. I am tired from traveling and would like to put on something clean."

Tehya opened the first basket and started looking for something to change into. She found a soft little pouch she did not recognize. "What is this?" she asked, holding it up.

"Oh. I nearly forgot. Open it." He smiled, anticipating her pleasure.

She quickly but carefully tipped the soft little hide sack and poured the contents into her other hand. "Oh!" she practically squealed. "It is so beautiful!" Not the same amber tones as her other necklace, this one sparkled with crystals that were almost clear.

"May I wear it now?" Her eyes sparkled.

"Of course. It is yours to do with as you wish." Khon'Tor walked over to help her put it on. "There. It is almost as beautiful as you, I have to admit. I must be sure to thank Oh'Dar again for the fine workmanship."

Tehya touched the necklace, admiring how it felt resting against her skin. Then she returned to unpacking their things.

Her fingers found another package, much bulkier. She picked up a wrapped hide tucked among the other items and unfolded it, revealing the Waschini blade Khon'Tor had almost used to kill himself.

"Adoeete," she said, turning and holding out the blade so he could see it.

"Here, let me have it, please," and he walked over and took it from her hands. "Do not be alarmed. I took a walk around Kthama before we left, and I found it in the grasses where I had dropped it."

He turned it in the sunlight, inspecting it more closely. A formidable weapon. *We have nothing like this. If this is representative of Waschini weaponry, then they are far ahead of us. The stories of the Waschini depict them as heartless, soulless marauders. Yet, what of Oh'Dar's positive example? If I cannot judge them all by Oh'Dar, how do I condemn them based on possibly inflated tales of their crimes? Have we not just learned an important lesson about the unreliability of stories passed from one to another? Where lies the truth of the Waschini?*

Khon'Tor wrapped the knife back in the protective rough hide, walked over to one of the walls near their sleeping mat, and reached up, searching for the cubby hole where items might be kept safely and secretly. Tehya had explained that every set of living quarters at the Far High Hills had this same arrangement.

Her eyes grew wide when she realized what he was doing.

After pushing it into the little opening, he walked back and kissed her sweetly on the lips. "I promise you, Saraste', you need have no fear of my using that against myself. Any thoughts I had of leaving this world at my own hand are forever gone."

Tehya spent the rest of the afternoon better familiarizing Khon'Tor with Amara. It took far longer than it should have as so many people stopped to talk to them, wanting to welcome Tehya back and to stand in the presence of the famous Khon'Tor of the High Rocks. Several of Tehya's friends had cornered them, and the females looked Khon'Tor up and down, not even trying to hide their admiration.

"I think your wraps are handsome, Adik'Tar. I hope you do not mind me saying that, Tehya," said one of her friends, staring at Khon'Tor. "I hope it is a trend that will catch on."

"Thank you, I also think they look fetching," Tehya said, the slightest frown on her face. When her friend reached out as if to touch the material, Tehya pulled Khon'Tor away from the circle of her friends. "We have to go," she called back as she led him away.

"Tomorrow, I will take you outside and show you all the places where my brothers and I played— including our secret hideaway where we would go and make up stories to entertain each other!"

As Tehya's parents had greeted Tehya and Khon'Tor, so had others been waiting to see Urilla Wuti. Iella, Drista—Iella's mother—and Urilla Wuti's Helper, Hollia, all warmly greeted the Healer.

"We are so glad you are back, Urilla Wuti. Are you staying for a while this time?" asked Drista as they embraced.

"Yes. I am looking forward to being home and also continuing to work with your daughter."

Hollia, too, embraced Urilla Wuti, saying she would be ready to meet whenever the Healer was.

"And who is this?" Drista asked, looking over at Nootau, who she noticed could not keep his eyes off her daughter.

"This is Nootau," explained Urilla Wuti, "the son of the new Leader of the High Rocks, Acaraho'Tor, and the Healer Adia'Mok. He will be visiting for a while. He also has an interest in learning about the practice of healing."

Iella stole a fleeting glance at Nootau before lowering her eyes.

Drista and Urilla Wuti walked ahead while Nootau and Iella walked together behind them.

"Do you know where you are staying, Nootau?" asked Iella, only briefly glancing at him as they walked.

"Harak'Sar said I would use the room I had last time, so I will be settled in quickly. Will you be at the evening meal?"

"Yes, with Mother and my aunt, no doubt. I trust you will join us?" she asked, this time directly smiling up at him.

"I would not miss it," he smiled back at her. They walked on a little until they came to Urilla Wuti's room.

Urilla Wuti sighed deeply, pausing a moment outside the door. "It is good to be home for more than a visit, I must say." She turned to the others. "I will see you at evening meal. For now, I am going to rest and spend some time in reflection."

Iella, Nootau, and Drista continued on to Nootau's room, and Iella's mother asked, "Tell me, Nootau, are you paired?"

"Mother!" Iella cried out, staring at her, wild-eyed.

Nootau chuckled, "No, I am not, though I am not against it. I have just not felt ready yet."

"Well, tomorrow, then, my daughter can show you around Amara. It is beautiful here. We are blessed to have a cave system nearly as large as Kthama. Our fields produce abundant crops, and there is more than enough bounty to get us through the colder months. The bees are plentiful and keep us in honey. The Great Spirit blesses us, and we have a good life here," Drista added.

"Mother, *please*," Iella begged.

"Oh, alright," laughed Drista as she left them. "I will see you both later."

Iella covered her face with her hands. "Please forgive her. She thinks because I am not paired that there is something wrong with me."

"*Is there*?" Nootau teased her.

Iella thumped his arm. "Nooooo," she laughed. "I am just particular. Like you, maybe," she teased back.

"Good. Hold out for what you want. I have seen what true love looks like, and I will settle for nothing less," he said as he stared down into her eyes. "And neither should you."

Iella blushed and turned away. "Come, I will take you the rest of the way to your room."

❂

Nootau stretched out on the sleeping mat and closed his eyes; it had been an emotionally difficult journey, and he was happy for some privacy. He immediately pictured Iella in his embrace, her soft lips pressing against his.

His eyes flew open. *What am I doing? Iella's life is here. She is one of the Healers of the Far High Hills. Even though it will be a long time before Urilla Wuti passes the full mantle to her, Iella would not leave. And Pan told me I had an important role to play in our people's future and that I was to look after and help An'Kru. How can I do that from here?*

Nootau tossed and turned awhile, fearing that the path his heart was coaxing him down could only end in heartbreak.

❂

Harak'Sar had arranged for a large table to be set aside for him at the evening meal. Iella, Urilla Wuti, Khon'Tor, and Tehya and her parents were gathered there together with Thorak, the High Protector. Nootau entered, led by Urilla Wuti's

Helper, who pointed out Harak'Sar's table and led him over.

"I apologize," he began. "I did not realize I was so tired, and I fell asleep. Luckily Hollia was on her way here and stopped by to fetch me."

"We have all been through a lot; it is no problem," said Harak'Sar.

"Sit here," suggested Iella, scooting over to make room next to her at the end of the bench. There was not quite enough room for him, and as Nootau slipped in beside her, he was unable to prevent his thigh from touching hers.

"Oops, sorry," he said. "It is a little tight."

Iella blushed and smiled.

Nootau looked up to see High Protector Thorak staring at him from across the smooth rock table.

They all passed the time with conversation.

"Khon'Tor," said Vosha, "Tehya's father and I want to acknowledge your sacrifice in stepping down from the leadership at the High Rocks to come and live here with us. I do not know exactly what to say, but we are in debt to you. It will, no doubt, be a huge adjustment."

"I have come to accept that change is the nature of life," Khon'Tor answered, "whether we welcome it or not. I do embrace this new period of my life with your daughter and Arismae, but I am a bit turned around, I will admit."

Tehya changed the subject, not wanting her mate to be put any further on the spot.

"Nootau is going to be studying with Iella while he is here," she said. "His mother is the Healer at the High Rocks, as I am sure you all know. So he has it in his blood."

"A male Healer?" Thorak scoffed.

"Well, that remains to be seen," said Tehya. "He has an interest in learning about the flowers, herbs, and roots, at least."

Nootau avoided looking in Thorak's direction; he was aware that the High Protector's iron glare was locked on him throughout the whole meal.

When it was over, everyone said good night and went on their way.

"I will see you in the morning, Nootau," Iella called out. "I promised you a tour, so do not sleep in," she teased. "Meet me at first light by the entrance."

Nootau nodded and took one last look at Thorak, who was tied up in conversation with Tehya's father, wondering if the High Protector had heard the exchange.

Harak'Sar turned to Khon'Tor. "If you have a moment, I need to speak with you and Tehya."

Harak'Sar waited until the others had left.

"At the High Rocks, you formed a Circle of Counsel, a small number of your community whose opinions and experience you sometimes called upon regarding important matters. I think that is a valuable idea and have said as much to the High Council. I suggested each Leader should consider forming his own Circle of Counsel."

Khon'Tor stood silently. Out of the corner of his eye, he could see Tehya looking up at him. *Where is this going?*

"I would like for you to sit on my Circle of Counsel," Harak'Sar said.

For a moment, Khon'Tor stared at the Leader. *What has turned things around between us? Harak'Sar's previous attitude was one of pronounced disdain.* "What would the High Council think of this?"

"It is not their decision," Harak'Sar answered. "You are known as one of the People's greatest Leaders. Your judgment and guidance have been key to bringing our people through these difficult times. To lose that insight would be foolish."

Khon'Tor could feel Tehya squeezing his hand. He feared that at any moment, she might start hopping up and down in excitement. He glanced at her briefly, and she quieted down a bit.

"I am honored at your faith in me. I believe it would bring you difficulty from the Overseer, however."

"Kurak'Kahn is no longer Overseer of the High Council."

Khon'Tor dug his nails into his free palm to hide his reaction. *When did this happen? And why? I assume no one told me because I am no longer part of the People's leadership. But now, with Harak'Sar's suggestion—*

"Please consider my invitation." Harak'Sar paused. "This is not a mercy offering. You must know by now that is not in my nature," he added.

"Thank you. It is generous and far more than I could have imagined," Khon'Tor said, before leading his mate away.

Once out of earshot, Tehya could contain her excitement no longer.

"Oh, Adoeete. This is an answered prayer. And everyone will benefit. Harak'Sar is right; it would be a terrible waste to lose your experience and wisdom."

Khon'Tor was gazing off into the distance.

"Tell me you are going to accept?" she cajoled.

He looked back down at her, seeing the joy lighting up her beautiful eyes. Her faith in him softened his resistance. "Most likely, I will, Saraste'. But I wonder what has happened to Kurak'Kahn, that he is no longer the Overseer, and who will be the next chosen?"

The next morning, Nootau met Iella as planned. She carried a colorful woven basket with a handle. "The last crop of raspberries is out. Want to help me pick some?"

Nootau offered to carry the basket, but she declined, and they went on their way.

"I have to ask you a question, please," said

Nootau as they walked. "Last night, the High Protector seemed unhappy that I was sitting next to you. Do you mind sharing what the story is there? Am I intruding somehow?"

"There is no story," she said. "Well, maybe, yes, there is. Thorak has liked me since we were offspring. We used to play together. He looked out for me like a big brother. When I was called to be a Healer, and it was forbidden that I pair, he became despondent and withdrawn. Then I realized that though I thought of him as a brother, he did not think of me as a sister. He finally came out of it, though."

"Forgive me, but it did not appear last night that he *came out of it*."

"Well, yes," she said, her hand lightly brushing the tops of the wildflowers along the path as they walked. "I should have said he did for a while—as if he had made peace with it. But then, when word came that Healers could be paired, and I did not encourage him in any way, he finally realized I did not feel the same toward him."

Nootau stooped over and picked a beautiful, lacy morning dancer. He presented her with the bloom.

She smiled at him as she took it and tucked the white flower into place behind one ear.

"We have never talked about it openly. I hate that it hurts Thorak, but you cannot help how you feel about someone, can you?" She stopped and turned to look up at Nootau.

He stopped walking and turned to her, "No. I do not believe you can." And he leaned over and briefly, ever-so-lightly, brushed his lips across hers.

Iella dropped the basket. She snaked her arms around Nootau's neck and raised herself up on her toes, pressing against him. He slipped his arms around her waist and pulled her tighter as their lips met in an impassioned kiss.

"What is going on here! Let her go!" a voice boomed from behind them.

Nootau released Iella and looked over to see Thorak scowling at him, muscles tensed and fists clenched.

"Thorak," Iella said. "Please. This is none of your business."

"No? Well, I am about to make it my business," he snapped. Turning to Nootau, he barked out, "What are you doing here? You do not belong at Amara. I suggest you get on your way back to the High Rocks before someone gets hurt."

"Is that a threat?" Nootau took a step forward, putting Iella behind him, and glared at Thorak.

"It is if you do not leave. Iella is not for you," hissed the High Protector.

"Excuse me," Iella stepped out from behind Nootau and faced Thorak. "You do not get any say in who I am or am not *for*. Seriously, Thorak. Let it go. I am sorry; I know you have feelings for me, and we should have talked about it long ago. I simply do not feel that way toward you. I care about you, but not in the way you want me to."

Thorak pulled a fallen branch out of the weeds, moved Iella aside, and threw it down, barely missing Nootau's feet.

"I warned you," he said.

"I am not afraid of you. And you are not going to bully me into leaving. I will be here for some time, so you had better get used to it," Nootau said, kicking the branch out of the way.

"Just go," Iella begged of Thorak. "Please."

"You do not even know him, and you let him kiss you? Put his hands on you? I watched you press yourself against him."

"I am sorry, Thorak. I'm sure this is difficult. I care about you, as I said, but I do not have the kind of feelings for you that draw the female to want to lie with the male."

"So you reject me but instead, you throw yourself at the first stranger who comes along," he sneered. "Is it because he is the son of the new Leader of the High Rocks?"

"That is unfair," Iella said, her brows furrowed tightly together. "If you do not know me any better than to think that matters to me, then it just further proves how we were never suited for each other."

"I have waited for you all this time, hoping you would come to your senses about me. Your mother favors our pairing; why are you so stubborn?"

"That is enough," said Nootau, stepping toward Thorak. "Leave her alone, or I will make you."

Thorak sized Nootau up, the muscled thighs, powerful biceps, the barrel chest. Though they each had about an even chance, he did not want to risk losing in front of Iella.

"Some other time, perhaps," he snarled and pushed past Nootau, purposefully using his shoulder to knock his rival off balance. Nootau righted himself and turned to watch Thorak storm off.

"That was uncomfortable," Nootau said, staring after him

"Yes. I am sorry," Iella answered.

"I meant for you. Not for me," Nootau said, glancing her way. "I am not worried about him. Oh, I feel bad that he cares for you as he does, knowing that he can never have you. It must be difficult to accept."

"Have you ever felt that way about a female?" she asked.

Nootau turned and looked down at her. Then he picked up the basket and wiped it off.

"No. I have many female friends, but I never before felt that way about anyone. Not like that, no. But I can imagine how it would hurt terribly not to have your affections returned."

They walked together in silence, shortly coming upon the raspberry patch. The berries were perfectly ripe, freely releasing themselves at a touch. Iella playfully threw some at Nootau, who turned it into a game and tried to catch them in his mouth. They laughed till their sides hurt.

After they had eaten as many berries as their stomachs could hold, and when Iella's basket was full to the brim, they walked down to the stream, and she showed him the best fishing spots. They sat together on the bank, washed the red stains from their hands and mouths, and splashed their feet in the water.

"My brother loves to swim," Nootau said.

"He does?" she chuckled. "That is unusual. I also enjoy it. But you males with your thick coats—understandably, you do not."

"Well, he is Waschini. He dries quickly," and they both laughed.

In a bold moment, Iella reached over and tugged at Nootau's loincloth. "What is this? Why do you wear it?" she asked.

"It is called a loincloth. The Brothers wear them. Surely you have seen them before?"

"A lying cloth? What is it lying about?" she teased.

"No," he laughed. "A *loy-in* cloth." Nootau leaned over and whispered in her ear, letting his breath warm her neck, "Trust me, there will never be lies between us."

A delicious warmth blossomed through her center, and she blushed at her own unabashed flirtation with this handsome, virile male.

For a while, they sat in silence together, pulling

some fading blossoms off the nearby plants, tossing them into the water, and watching them float away.

"Nootau, what do you think about An'Kru?" she asked quietly.

"What do *you* think about him? What did you think when you first saw him?"

"I did not know what to think. He has so much more hair-covering than any of us, and he is so very young. And it is almost silver. Other than that, he looks normal. Well, except for his eyes. They are almost dark grey, like the winter storm clouds, but with light shining through them. From the moment he was born, when he looked at you, it felt as if he were looking into your soul. So peculiar for an offspring. Or anyone, really. You cannot help but love An'Kru, though. There is something exceptional about him, and it is not just his coloring."

"I have to protect him," Nootau said, looking off into the distance. "I have to look after him. I looked after Oh'Dar when we were growing up. Thorak is not the first bully I have had to face; there was one at the High Rocks. Kahrok. For some reason, he seemed to hate Oh'Dar. I had many run-ins with him."

"What finally happened? Did he just grow out of tormenting your brother?"

"He slacked off after a while. But no, actually, our Leader, Khon'Tor, expelled him from the community. But not for picking on Oh'Dar. So even though that resolved it, I learned that bullies are pretty much alike. They usually step down when you stand up to them."

"Usually?" she asked.

"Well, yes," he chuckled. "They do not always step down. I have had some knockdown, drag-out fights with Kahrok in my time, it is true. But the important thing is that it was kept between him and me, and no harm came to my brother. And that is what I have to make sure of for An'Kru too."

"I understand what you are saying," she said solemnly. Then she got up. "I think we should head back. My aunt will be looking for me by now, I am sure."

Nootau stood and flicked a stone across the water, causing it to skip several times.

They walked back to Amara in silence.

That evening, Iella did not join them at Harak'Sar's table. Nootau spent the meal hoping she would come. When she did not, he went to his quarters with a heavy heart.

## CHAPTER 3

Acaraho, Adia, Nimida, and Tar stood in the shadows a safe distance away. The clacking of rocks echoed against the walls to the end of the bleak tunnel in which they were standing. Having spent days shoring up the unstable area, Haan and several of his males were now busy clearing away the rubble which had collapsed over Tar's sister Lifrin, burying her so many years ago. Dust billowed and filled the air as the giant Sarnonn easily lifted boulders and stacked them out of the way.

Finally, they had cleared the pile. Haan stooped down, gingerly gathered up Lifrin's remains, and placed them on a soft deer skin before folding them safely inside. He then carried them back to where Acaraho and the others were standing.

"I am sorry for the loss of one so dear to you," Haan said to Tar, as he respectfully cradled the precious bundle. "But I am honored that we could help your sister have a proper Good Journey."

Nimida put an arm around Tar and hugged him tightly to her side.

"Thank you," Tar said. "It means a lot."

Haan nodded and addressed Acaraho, "They will replace the boulders respectfully and make sure that the area is still structurally sound before they leave."

"Thank you, Haan," Acaraho replied. "We will quarter off this area more securely. It is, after all, sacred ground. It should remain undisturbed."

Haan slowly carried all that was left of Lifrin past Adia, Nimida, and Tar, who then followed him back out of the deep recesses of Kthama. Nimida's eyes brimmed with tears; her heart was breaking to see Tar having all the pain of his sister's death dredged up again, even though, in the end, it would perhaps help him find peace.

Later, they held the ceremony, Nimida once again standing at Tar's side and comforting him. Gathered around were Mapiya, Adia, Nadiwani, Haan, and those Sarnonn who had helped unearth Lifrin's remains.

Acaraho spoke. "Many years ago, a brave young Healer gave her life to save others. She was called down to ease the passing of one of my crew, Irka, who had gotten caught in a cave-in. We all knew Irka would not make it, as did Lifrin. But having the Healer's heart, she tried to relieve his suffering. While she was ministering to him, a larger rockslide was about to take place. Sensing its coming and knowing that if others were to try to save her, they would be crushed, she shouted out for them to get out while they could. Because of her warning, the other males there escaped with their lives. I was one of them."

"Lifrin's sacrifice saved my life as well as the life of our former Leader, Khon'Tor. But she left behind a little brother, Tar, whom we all know. Decades later, thanks to our brothers and neighbors, the Sarnonn, we are now finally able to give her a proper ceremony."

Everyone looked at Haan and his followers in appreciation.

Tar stepped forward to speak. "After we lost our parents, my sister became mother and father to me. She was all I had. The day I lost her, what little was left of my world came to an end. I do not know how I survived her death, though I know I owe a debt of gratitude both to Acaraho and Khon'Tor, who made sure I was looked after and provided for.

Tar stopped a moment to collect himself.

"So now I am standing here saying goodbye once more to my beloved sister, finally able to end the heartache from all these years of knowing that she was buried in the dark under those cold boulders. And thanks to the continued kindness of Acaraho and Adia, who have welcomed me into their circle and their hearts, I feel I am no longer so alone in the world.

"And because Adia would not give up on me, I

have been able to risk caring about someone again," and Tar looked at Nimida. "I can now embrace a new possibility for myself. One of a life filled with love, companionship, and joy."

Adia looked over at Nimida, whose eyes were shining with tears.

"So, as a chapter of my life is finally closing, I wish for a new chapter to open. And I would ask for you to carry a message to the High Council, please Adik'Tar Acaraho, that Nimida of the Great Pines and I wish to be paired."

Nimida wrapped her arms around Tar. He leaned over and rested his head on hers.

Adia said a quiet prayer of thanks. She went over to Nimida and hugged her. "Your mother will be so glad; she knows you have found happiness here." Then she added for Tar, "As, I am certain, does Lifrin." They hugged again, and Adia squinted to cut off the tears before they could start. She glanced at Acaraho, and he nodded, giving her a sweet smile.

Slowly everyone else congratulated the couple, thanked Haan and his followers again, and left the burial place to Tar and Nimida.

When Acaraho, Adia, and the others had made it back to Kthama, Nadiwani stopped them. "We— Mapiya, Awan, and I—have a surprise for you, Adia," she said.

"A surprise?"

"Yes. Come with us."

Nadiwani started leading them down an all too familiar tunnel. Adia stopped partway to their destination.

"Oh, no," she said. "No. I am not ready."

"Oh, yes," said Nadiwani. "It is time. It is time to move forward." She took her friend's hand and tugged her back into motion.

They walked the rest of the way, and shortly Acaraho and Adia were standing in the doorway of the Leader's Quarters.

Adia stepped inside, looked around, and gasped. The entire area had been transformed. The walls were washed in chalk that had been tinted just barely with a soothing shade of lavender, and beautiful new arrangements of dried flowers hung from the overhead ventilation shafts.

A brand-new sleeping mat had been placed in a different area than that used by Khon'Tor and Tehya. The softsit had also been moved to the other side of the room. A faint scent of burnt sage filled the air.

Though it was hard to believe possible, it truly no longer resembled the quarters of the previous Leader.

"Look here," said Mapiya, walking over to the far end. "This is An'Kru's new nest!"

Acaraho walked over to examine it. "Thank you."

Adia joined him. "It is perfect. So cozy and inviting. Thank you for everything you have done here."

"We did not bring your personal things or Acara-ho's Leader's Staff," said Nadiwani. "We know that only the Leader may lay hands on it."

Acaraho nodded.

"I am ready to have everything else moved when-ever you say," Awan added.

Acaraho looked at Adia. "Thank you. But I will take care of bringing our things over. Then, after we have had a day or so to settle in, I would like to call together the Circle of Counsel that Khon'Tor created. I expect you all to attend."

"We will be honored," nodded Awan, speaking for everyone.

"I am sure you want your son back," said Mapiya. "Let me go and collect him from Pakuna. I will return shortly."

Before long, Adia and Acaraho were alone in the Leader's Quarters.

"Who would have believed any of this?" she asked.

"From the moment Khon'Tor assigned me to protect you, Saraste'," he said, "I knew where I belonged. Even though I could never be with you as I wanted, I accepted it as my fate. My heart was lost to you. I could never be with anyone else, and if that meant I had to live a life of celibacy, then I would somehow find the strength to do it. I resigned myself to being satisfied with the memory of the days I spent holding you as you were recovering from Khon'Tor's attack. And I prayed, though I could never tell you, that in a hundred little ways you would somehow feel my love for you and know that I would do everything in my power to prevent any harm coming to you again."

"And I you, my love," she said. "There were so many things I wanted to tell you that I knew I would never get to say. How much I admired you and looked up to you. That at your side, I felt safe, protected, even loved. That if I had not been the Healer, you would have been my only choice. I felt trapped in a nowhere place of infinite longing, unable to claim you as my own, yet unable to let you go. I suffered, seeing no way for us ever to be together, and I feared that you felt the same way and that those feelings would keep you from the life you deserved. A life shared with a female you loved, a family of your own."

She paused, "And look at us now. We must never forget where our journey has led us. We have seen one miracle after another. Who knows what tomorrow will bring?"

Acaraho and Adia sat in the same meeting room Khon'Tor had always used for his Circle of Counsel meetings. With them were Awan, Mapiya, and Nadi-wani. Adia gently rocked An'Kru.

"So. Here we are," the new Leader said. "I do not think any of us could have seen this coming. I know I have said it before, and I will say it again; I did not seek the leadership of the High Rocks. If you had told me that any of the events of the past few years would take place, I would have told you it was impossible. Now, Awan, Mapiya, what is the pulse of the community?"

"It is too soon to tell how long it will take for them to adjust," said Mapiya. "But in my opinion, people are still reeling. Do not take it personally, Acaraho. From the time of Hakani's return, through the Sarnonn sickness when we lost so many of our males, with the opening of Kthama Minor, and because of the Sarnonn rebels, the forced evacuation to other communities. And now this? It feels as if there is no solid foundation left."

Adia closed her eyes to take a moment, until An'Kru cooed and grasped her little finger.

"And the events around An'Kru's birth," Mapiya added.

"As far as the males are concerned," said Awan, "they will have no problem with your being the Leader. They have followed your leadership for as long as they can remember. To them, it will not be that much different."

"That is true, to a point," said Acaraho. "But that brings up a subject we need to discuss. Since I am no longer the High Protector, I am appointing Awan to that position in my stead. That means, Awan, that you will, in turn, have to select a First Guard."

Awan nodded. "I am honored by your trust in me.

I will give you several names to consider, those I would recommend, and we can decide together."

"As you wish," Acaraho answered.

Adia looked around the room, "This group seems so much smaller now. Khon'Tor and Tehya are gone, and also Urilla Wuti, and Oh'Dar is away. I suspect Oh'Dar will now be away as much as he is here. I hope teaching Whitespeak is not placing too much on his shoulders."

Nadiwani spoke up, "Acaraho, have you considered having Nootau join the Circle? I know it is a long way off, but he is first in line to your leadership."

"I will have to think about it," he answered, looking over at his mate. "The Circle is small, to be sure, and it would behoove him to be part of the conversations. I just do not know yet if it is prudent at this juncture. I do know that I need to start meeting regularly with Haan. I have considered asking him to let the People see the Chamber of the Ancients before it is sealed up again forever."

"All of them?" asked Nadiwani.

"It would be a lot to ask and to organize. But I do not want the truth to drift into folklore. The more who see it first-hand, the longer the truth has a chance of being kept alive." Acaraho rested his face in his hands. "The High Council was clearly shaken by it; I could see it in their faces. And they did not discuss it afterward, other than the Overseer's remarks—which were telling enough on their own."

"Speaking of Kthama Minor, perhaps we need our own Wall of Records," said Awan, absent-mindedly.

"The record keepers already have that—as such. They use it to work out the pairings, even though it only goes back a few generations. But you are correct. When he turned over the leadership of Kthama, Khon'Tor said that the point of learning Whitespeak was to give us a detailed way of recording history. We must start *writing down* the events of the past decades. All we have experienced must be written down, giving us a written record of the history, so it is not preserved only through storytelling. I cannot think where we would start recording the events; we have no large chamber not being used, but perhaps we will come up with something."

Acaraho then asked Mapiya for a general report.

"We are nearing the high harvest time. We have had a bountiful year and should have no trouble filling the stores. Soon, the oldest offspring will start gathering the crops and stocking the Gnoaii. Nadi-wani has offered to take charge of the offspring's efforts this year, so she can also oversee the proper picking and storage of the medicinals the Healers need."

Adia mouthed a thank you to Nadiwani.

"On another front, Nimida has become one of our best toolmakers. She and Tar have been busy honing our hunting spears and blades, and replacing any which are no longer usable," Mapiya continued.

"They are also making writing tools as Oh'Dar has shown them how to do. They seem happy in their work."

"What else?" asked Acaraho.

"As for the change in leadership, I have heard no negative remarks. But they are reeling from losing Khon'Tor, and it will take them some while to adjust. They do, however, like the loincloth and upper wrap you have been wearing. They were also complimentary about Nootau's wraps. As you have seen, even though they do not need to, some of the adult males are copying him. With Tehya gone, we will need someone else to develop new designs because they have really caught on with the females. Even more so, if the young males start wanting to wear coverings. As far as An'Kru is concerned, they are fascinated with him and cannot get enough of seeing him. Every day, so many ask me how he is doing."

Adia nodded—curiosity about him was to be expected.

Acaraho sat quietly, waiting for Mapiya to finish before he addressed her. "You have been the female's organizer and spokesperson for some time now. There is no official title for the role you play, but there should be."

"Thank you," she said humbly. "But I do not need a title."

"Maybe not, but you deserve one all the same. I will try to come up with something, or if you think of one, please let me know. Do not be shy."

"You might ask Haan," suggested Awan. "I know they have a term for the Fixer, the one who is skilled in repairs and innovative new ideas. Perhaps they have other titles we could incorporate."

Adia looked up from admiring her offspring. "That is a great idea. We have a whole culture to learn from. We have common roots, but it seems obvious we have lost the Mothoc customs and knowledge. We need someone who would be interested in learning directly from the Sarnonn. And perhaps we can do the same for them?"

"Like an exchange? A cultural exchange of some type?" asked Nadiwani.

"Yes, exactly," Adia smiled.

"I support that," said Acaraho. "It will help us to enrich our knowledge with theirs. No doubt, much more has been lost to us than we realize. That would also leave me free to concentrate on forging the bond between our people at a leadership level. "

" I am sorry Oh'Dar could not stay longer," Nadiwani said to Adia.

"He needed to return to Acise and the Brothers' village. As I said, I hope this is not wearing on him. It is ironic; for so long, he did not know where he belongs, and now he belongs in two places. I wonder if that is any easier." She smiled wistfully.

"Three places," pointed out Nadiwani, "if you count Shadow Ridge."

Acise watched happily as her life-walker, Oh'Dar, and her brother, sister, and parents sat discussing the state of the village. She had never been so happy. If she had any worries at all, it was the continued disappearance of Pajackok and what the future might hold when, and if he returned.

"Stores will be full for the winter, which the signs indicate will be a rough one," said Honovi.

"We are in good shape for now," agreed Chief Is'Taqa. "There is much to be done, and we need every able-bodied person we have helping to complete the winter preparations."

Acise saw tension crease Oh'Dar's brow.

"Speak, please," she said, realizing that whatever was bothering him was also difficult for him to say out loud. "I can see something is troubling you."

"I feel I need to return to Shadow Ridge," he finally admitted, eyes downcast. "I have been gone long enough for my grandparents to be worried. They are older, and it is difficult having no way to tell them what is going on or when I will be back. Or anything about my life here, really."

"Would they be happy to know you are bonded?" asked Honovi.

"Oh, I think so. I believe it would do them good to know I am not alone and have found love and companionship."

"If you need to go back, then you must go," said Acise softly, placing her hand on Oh'Dar's forearm.

"I wish you could go with me, but we know you

cannot," he said, looking her in the eye. "I used to daydream about taking you back with me. I would love you to meet them, to experience that part of who I am. But it would be foolhardy and not worth the risk."

Acise interlaced her arm with his and leaned into him.

Is'Taqa turned to Oh'Dar, "When will you leave?"

"Soon."

"I want to go!" said Noshoba.

"No," said his father. "You are far too young, for one thing."

"Is it because the Waschini are bad?" the young boy asked.

Honovi took Noshoba's hand and drew him over to stand in front of her. "No," she answered. "You know the Waschini are not all bad. Oh'Dar is Waschini. Your grandmother was Waschini, and I grew up among them. It is not fair to say that a group of people are all bad or all good. Look at our village; we have our own problems among ourselves," she added. And everyone knew she was referring to Pajackok's fight with Oh'Dar.

"Has anyone seen or heard from Pajackok?" asked Acise.

"Tac'agawa tells me they know nothing of where he went. The People's watcher saw him head to the west out of our territory. He has not been gone that long, though I know his parents are worried."

That evening, Oh'Dar and Acise sat together in their new shelter and discussed the matter further.

"Are you sure I could not go with you?" Acise asked. "I know it is important to you."

"Saraste'," he said, using the People's endearment, "the last thing I would do is put the Brothers in harm's way. It was just a daydream, a way to try to weave the three parts of who I am together in some small way. I will go back and tell them I am now bonded, and they will be happy to know I am not alone. But it is hard for them that I disappear into a void of their understanding of where and how I live. I know they suspect it is with the Brothers, but they do not know for sure, and they have been respectful about not asking. The Waschini world must not know where I have been all this time."

Oh'Dar rested his head in his hands.

Acise ran her hand down the back of his hair to soothe him.

"The only places I feel I belong are here with you and at Kthama. But I have this other place where part of my heart is. And I cannot reconcile the three."

"What if they came here to live with us? Is that a possibility?"

Oh'Dar raised his eyes and looked at her.

"What?" he asked, frowning.

"What if your grandparents, you know who I

mean, came here and became part of your life here? Would they do it?"

Oh'Dar straightened up and turned to her.

"I cannot imagine it. That would mean giving up everything they know there. How would they adjust? I doubt they are ready to live as we do; they are used to far more comforts than we have."

"You do not know if you do not ask them," she said quietly.

Oh'Dar shook his head. "That would be asking too much."

"I cannot stand seeing you like this. All you ever wanted is peace and a sense of belonging. And now it seems you have unrest wherever you are. I think you should at least ask them," Acise said. "You have mentioned that they are older. If you wait too long, there will be no chance of their making that kind of adjustment. And one of these days, when you go back, it will be too late; one—or both of them—will be gone. And if you ask them, you will know you gave them the chance to decide for themselves."

Oh'Dar sighed deeply. "I will think about it," was all he said.

The next morning, Oh'Dar announced he would need to go back to Kthama before leaving for Shadow Ridge. "I must spend some time with my parents and check on the Whitespeak students. I will stop on my way back and say goodbye." He kissed her. "I do not know how long I will be."

Oh'Dar wanted to stretch his legs and had decided to walk back to Kthama rather than take Storm. He knew the watchers would send word he was on his way, and unless they had urgent tasks to attend to, no doubt his parents would assemble in time for his arrival.

The warm summer morning brought out all the scents of the forest. His journey was sweetened by the scent of pine, the smell of the soil, moist from the morning dew, and the fragrance from the wildflowers occasionally carried on the breeze. The sun shone through the woven canopy of leaves overhead, and when he could glimpse it, the sky was a beautiful blue. As he walked, chipmunks scurried across the path in front of him. Butterflies darted from blossom to blossom, brightly colored wings adding to the quiet beauty that surrounded him.

*Something has to give. I cannot keep living like this. No matter where I am, I feel I should be somewhere else. If I am at Kthama teaching Whitespeak, I feel guilty for not being with Acise and helping Chief Is'Taqa. If I am with Acise, I feel guilty about not being with my grandparents and worry about their getting further on in years. When I am at Shadow Ridge— It does not matter where I am; there is always the pressure to be elsewhere. Is there any chance Acise is right? Would they possibly come here and live with us? It is one thing to go from this life to the Waschini world with all its advantages, but to leave that world and come here? I did not realize how primitively we lived because I had no comparison. But now, I know. It feels like it is too much to ask. It is a preposterous idea. And so many things could go wrong.*

Oh'Dar continued in silence, mulling over Acise's idea until he could not think about it anymore. *Even though it seems too far-fetched to consider seriously, I will put it aside for now and ask Mother and Father. They are older; perhaps they can give me a more informed answer as to whether it is even fair to put my grandparents in that position and if I should even bring it up as a possibility.*

His mother was waiting for him at Kthama's entrance, cradling An'Kru.

"What is wrong? Something is troubling you," Adia immediately said. She put an arm around Oh'Dar's neck and hugged him.

"I must return to Shadow Ridge for a while. This is so hard, Mama. I need to be in three places at once."

"When are you leaving?"

"In a couple of days. I want to check on the students, see you, and get my Waschini clothes and boots."

Adia walked with him to his quarters.

"Acise said something last night; what if my Waschini family would come here and live with us?"

Adia stopped. "With us here at Kthama? Or with you and Acise at the Brothers' village?"

"I do not know. Either. Oh, it does not matter; I

could not possibly ask my grandparents to do that. Can you imagine what they would think?" He laughed at himself and shook his head. "It is a preposterous idea."

Adia looked at her son carefully. "I know you well enough to know that in some part of your mind, you are considering it."

"Only because of my own selfishness. Only because it would make my life easier to have everyone I love in one spot. And because each time I leave them, I worry I may not see them again. And each time I leave here, I worry the same about you."

"They may feel the same way. When you are gone, they worry about you, and when you are there, they are happy to have you with them, but they, too, must know you are torn. Perhaps it is not such a terrible idea, at least to consider."

"But Second Law forbids having contact with Outsiders."

"Yes, and no one knows that better than I," she answered. "But we have also learned that what we believe to be carved in stone may not be so, after all. I think you should at least propose it to your father. Times are changing, like it or not."

After first meal, Oh'Dar sat for a while with his parents. When Acaraho had heard Oh'Dar out, he decided to convene his Circle of Counsel.

A bit later, Acaraho stood to address his advisors and explained what Oh'Dar was struggling with.

"Here?" asked High Protector Awan. "You want to bring these Waschini here to live at Kthama?" Then he looked at Oh'Dar, "No offense."

Oh'Dar waved his hand, "None taken. They are Waschini, after all. There is no disparagement in speaking the truth."

"I agree you cannot take Acise to meet them," said his father. "For one thing, while your grandparents may accept your association with the Brothers, that does not mean the others they know would feel the same. It could bring trouble down on you, which might easily follow you back to the village. Secondly, since you have not told them of your life among the People, and they assume you were raised among the Brothers, if they came to live there, everyone at the village would continually have to dodge questions or lie to cover the truth."

"It would be a risk," said Nadiwani.

"And against Second Law," added Oh'Dar, "I know."

"It would be a risk, as much for them as for us," said Acaraho. "I agree with Nadiwani. But I believe that you have to take the chance and present the idea to them. After adjusting to our partnership with the Sarnonn, the People can surely accept two older Waschini. It is *their* adjustment I am worried about."

"I think they could get used to us. We are larger than them and the Brothers, but we do not look *all* that much different. It is the Sarnonn who might scare them half to death," said Adia.

"Do you think you could make them understand what a huge adjustment it would be? And that it would be a one-way trip. If they came, they would have to agree they could never leave. And even if they wanted to, no one would be allowed to help them find their way back. We are far, far away from any established Waschini routes. They would die of exposure before they could find their way to any Waschini encampment. They would have to understand and accept that reality fully. On that, there can be no negotiation," said Acaraho.

Adia became quiet before speaking again. "You know, they could help with your school." She looked across at Oh'Dar. "It would help take the pressure off you of having to do it all by yourself. And it would give them a purpose here."

"Yes," nodded Oh'Dar, "and Ben knows a lot about horse breeding. He might be able to help Yuma'qia and Bidzel in determining how best to diversify our bloodlines. I mean, it would take a while for them to learn our language, but Ben would bring a wealth of knowledge about bloodlines and how they work. At least with horses. The patterns must be similar."

Acaraho weighed in. "If we are even considering allowing them to live at Kthama, we must take it to the High Council. The Second Law tells us to have no contact with Outsiders. Even beyond that, it could potentially affect all our communities. There is much to consider."

Acaraho looked over at his mate, but she was distracted by An'Kru, who was fussing a bit.

"If we are to consider this at all, I need to know who supports proposing it to the High Council," Acaraho continued. "And who would vote to abandon the idea right here?"

Everyone indicated their consent to move forward, as outrageous as the concept sounded, and Oh'Dar let out a huge sigh.

"Before you travel to Shadow Ridge, I suggest I send a message to Urilla Wuti at the Far High Hills and request a High Council meeting. It will be up to you, son, to make your case on its merits," Acaraho said.

Acaraho had moved all his and Adia's belongings to the Leader's Quarters, except for their sleeping mat, which had not yet been discarded. Later that afternoon, while Oh'Dar busied himself with his students and Mapiya was watching An'Kru, Adia lay down in the safety of their old quarters.

She swept her eyes over what had been their home for several years now.

*I am not really ready to leave here—so many sweet memories. The first time I visited Acaraho in the Dream State and we lovemated, unaware until the next morning that it was not real. The first time we mated after we were paired. Long nights in each other's arms, sharing our hopes and longings. It feels as if the turmoil has been nonstop ever since we first met Haan. This was the place where we could have peaceful time alone together to dream our dreams.*

She sighed. *I know that in time, the Leader's Quarters will feel like home. But for now, this is where I feel most comfortable. I wonder how Urilla Wuti is settling in back at the Far High Hills. And Nootau.*

After a while, Adia felt a familiar pull. *E'ranale.* She relaxed her body, quieted her mind, and allowed herself to enter the Corridor.

As always, she was surrounded by beauty and infused with a sense of being alive that was unparalleled in Etera's realm. She took in the crystal-clear air, the celestial sounds of the songbirds, the delicious feel of the grass under her feet. She waited for E'ranale, welcoming whatever it was that the sage wanted to teach her.

The air changed, suddenly tinged with exuberance. Adia felt almost lightheaded, something she had never before experienced in the Corridor. Then a figure, even larger than E'ranale, began to materialize in front of her. Had she been on Etera, Adia would have been afraid, but instead, she was intrigued and drawn to the essence taking form in front of her.

Slowly the figure solidified, and Adia stifled a gasp. Standing in front of her was what looked like the embodiment of life itself. Her eyes followed from the ground up, a mammoth body covered in silver-white hair, iridescent, as if lit from within. Visible even under the luxuriant coat, the thighs, the arms, every part was rippled with contour that portrayed incredible strength. Vitality emanated from the form, and Adia felt all her experiences augmented far beyond what she ordinarily experienced in the Corridor.

Finally, Adia's eyes met those of the other, and in an instant, she knew the name, the one who had saved her while she was trying to rescue Khon'Tor and Tehya from their journey into krell.

*Pan.*

Adia waited silently, in awe. Pan smiled and said, " I am sorry my appearance here startles you."

"I am not really startled," Adia said, almost apologetic. "Perhaps. I am not sure. You are Pan."

"Yes."

"The last of the Mothoc Guardians."

"Yes," Pan nodded.

"Why have you brought me here?"

"I thought it was time we met. I know you have questions now that An'Kru has arrived."

Adia swallowed hard. "I am afraid I will fail him."

"Why?" Pan frowned. "Because he is different? This is not the first different Offspring you will have raised."

"No. Well, yes. Because I feel he has a destiny to

fulfill. And I am afraid I will not be up to giving him all he needs. That I will let him down."

"Every one of us has a destiny, and fear is always the enemy. Fear makes us doubt ourselves, doubt others, doubt what we know. Right now, you are fearful of many things, but I assure you they are all illusions that you have manufactured in your own mind. You know that it would not be given to you to do if you were not able to accomplish it."

"Yes," Adia admitted quietly. "Deep inside, I believe that."

"Then, when these fears surface, you must go deep inside. You have been guided. You will be guided. You are always guided. Even when things seem to be out of place, somewhere deep down, the Order of Functions is still engaged."

"But terrible things have happened. Painful things. How do I know tragedy will not befall An'Kru —due to my shortcomings?" Adia asked.

"Look to your left, Adia," Pan said, "and tell me what you see?"

"A row of locust trees, and beyond them, a field of the most vibrant and beautiful flowers I have ever seen."

"Past that," Pan said.

Adia looked around. "The horizon."

"And can you see what is beyond the horizon?"

"No."

"Your realm is filled with horizons. Because you are living in time, you have a limited view of events.

You cannot see beyond what is happening, much as you cannot see beyond the horizon over there. You cannot see the interconnection that is always taking place beyond your comprehension and imagination. Whether you know it or not, things are unfolding as they should."

"What you do not see is already seen and compensated for by the Order of Functions," she continued.

"I will never understand this." Adia closed her eyes.

"You will. One day, when you stand here beside me forever, free from time, it will all make sense. Until then, you must learn to trust that which you cannot see. You must have—"

"Faith," Adia said. "My whole life seems to be a lesson about learning to have faith."

"It is so with everyone. That is part of your journey on Etera. We must trust what we cannot see, what we cannot understand. We must trust that no matter what, no matter how painful, how challenging, life is unfolding around us in the most beneficent way possible for our soul's paths."

"Is the Order of Functions part of the One-Who-Is-Three?"

"The Three-Who-Are-One encompass everything. There is nothing separate from That Which Is. My mother, E'ranale, has spoken of this to you before."

Just then, a bird landed on Pan's shoulder. She

reached up, and it flitted to her outstretched finger. She lowered her hand, extending it to Adia.

In turn, Adia raised her hand, and the beautiful little creature hopped on to her finger. Adia stared transfixed. Its shining blue feathers had a depth of color that modulated, changed, and rippled in front of her eyes.

"Tell me about your friend, Adia," Pan said softly.

"She is beautiful. The most beautiful thing I have ever seen."

"Describe her to me. What are you experiencing?"

"I can feel the slightest weight of her, the press of her little toes curled around my finger. Her feathers look so soft, as fine as can be. She smells like the rich soil after a sweet summer rain. Her bright eyes are looking up at me as if both asking a question and answering it."

Suddenly, the little bird let out a string of song.

"Oh. That was beautiful, so lilting and haunting, yet consoling at the same time." Adia closed her eyes to listen further before asking, "Is it significant that she is a blue bird? The same bird my mother saw in her dream before I was born. And the same bird that is painted on the wall of the chamber where your—" Adia stopped.

"Anoww comes to tell us that a great blessing is approaching, just as Ravu'Bahl, the black crow, comes to remind us of our duty to Sacred Law. Much of the Mothoc wisdom and knowledge has been lost to the People, but much was preserved in the Sarnonn culture. It will be restored to you through them, as your ways become interwoven."

The little bird flew off, and Adia watched it until she could trace its flight no further.

Movement from Pan brought her back, and she turned to see the Guardian holding out a piece of fruit.

"Now, tell me about this."

Adia extended her palm, and Pan dropped the fruit into her hand.

"It is firm, and a beautiful deep red with a glossy shine that surpasses explanation. I can feel its weight as I hold it; there is a satisfying shape and solidity to it. I can tell from the rich smell that it is ripe and ready to eat." She looked back up at Pan for acknowledgment.

"Now, separate the weight and the beautiful red color, and the sweet fragrance."

Adia frowned. "I do not understand. I do not know how to do that. They are all part of the whole."

"Exactly. Just as the attributes that make up an apple cannot be separated out, neither can the attributes of All That Is. You perceive the apple as separate from everything else, but in reality, nothing is separated. It is all connected, at a level our minds cannot comprehend." She paused a moment for Adia to take in what she had just been told.

"Because we perceive separation, does not mean it is real. Any more than your perceiving of the horizon, the farthest your eyes can see, means there is nothing beyond it."

Adia looked over to the horizon, taking in what Pan was trying to tell her.

"So, to answer your question, the Order of Functions is an aspect of the One-Who-Is-Three. Yes. There are many names for our creator. The closest I can explain the Order of Functions is that it is the underlying intricate orchestration of the Great Mind, made manifest through the intention of the Great Will, and infused with the loving benevolence of the Great Heart, that works at an infinite level for the ultimate good of all creation."

Adia was gazing into the distance, trying to take in what she was hearing.

"It is a difficult concept to understand—how there is only the One Creation, yet we perceive its attributes as separate and disconnected. Even the concept of the Three-Who-Are-One alludes to separation where there is none. The act of creation is one orchestration. The Waschini have a term they use for it, the Universe, though they do not think of it this way, and it would help them if they did. Broken up, their word, uni-verse, means *the one song*."

There was a pause before Adia said, "Pan—my son, Oh'Dar—"

"The Waschini offspring you raised as your own. He is going back to Shadow Ridge soon, with the thought of bringing his family to Kthama. And you are concerned about the effect more Waschini would have on your community."

Adia nodded.

"Again, my mother has spoken to you about the threat of the Waschini, which comes from their belief in lack, which drives competition and ultimately becomes a self-fulfilling belief. Let us go back to the birds for a moment. How many different birds can you name for me?"

Adia started naming them. "There is the brown nester, the red-crested early comer, the skydiver, and the blue bird whom you called Anoww, who just flew off.

"How do you tell them apart?"

"By their size, their color, their song," Adia answered.

"Yet they are all thought of as birds, correct? Even though there is much variation between them?"

Adia nodded.

"So it is with the Waschini. Just as there is variation in the birds, there is variation in the Waschini. So far, the term is only used to reference the light-skinned ones who live in your local area. But there are others, Adia. Others who have darker skins, lighter skins, some with black hair—like the Brothers. Some with hair the color of the a'Pozz blossoms."

"Orange hair?"

"Yes, Adia. The Brothers, the Waschini, and those you have never seen are all the same in the way the birds are the same. I think of them as the Hue'Mahns."

"Hue'Mahns? Are you telling me the Brothers and the Waschini are the same; Hue'Mahns?"

"In the same way there are different birds, different fish, in the same way that one type of bird might be able to fly higher compared to the next, one fish might be more brightly colored than the next, they are different, yet the same—yes."

"But the Brothers are kind. The Brothers honor the Great Mother. They live in harmony with her and her creatures. That is not what we have heard about the Waschini."

"I realize that. But you must also understand that you cannot generalize about an entire population from the acts of a few. There are Waschini who are in tune with Etera, who respect her and care for her and all her creatures. And there are those who do not. The problem comes from the proportion. The more the negative beliefs permeate through and saturate the human population, the greater the risk to Etera."

"We are also part Hue'Mahn then because the Ancients bred with the Brothers."

"Yes. Tell me, until recently, has there been much strife among your people?"

"No. We have not before experienced the discord, the crimes, that have taken place recently."

"As the distorted human beliefs propagate, there will be more discord, more crime, more strife throughout Etera. Your people are not immune because the distortion caused by beliefs and actions affects the Aezaiterian stream after it has entered Etera."

"You are supposed to come and teach the new Sarnonn Guardians how to cleanse the flow of the Aezaitera."

"At the appointed time, yes. That and more."

"When? And where?" Adia's eyes grew wide. "Will you teach them on Etera? Or here in the Corridor?"

"The answers to your questions do not matter right now. I have already given you much to ponder."

"Will Urilla Wuti have this information too? I miss her," Adia confessed."

"I know you miss Urilla Wuti, and yes, I have already shared this with her. For now, it is best that you are brought here individually. Urilla Wuti has trained others before you, and now she needs to concentrate on her work with Iella. But of all her students, you are the best one, Adia. In time, the best student will surpass even the best teacher."

Adia frowned, unable to imagine being more adept than Urilla Wuti.

"It is time for you to return to your realm. Do not worry, I will join you soon enough. Until then, work on calming your mind's constant rattling of worries and problems. An'Kru is where he needs to be. And you are enough; you are more than enough to help him achieve his destiny. His coming has already brought softening to those whose hearts are open to his influence, to the very pure vibration of his soul. And the older he gets the greater will be his influence on Etera."

At Pan's last words, a great peace welled up, around, and through Adia, and then she felt herself return to Etera and became aware once more of lying on the sleeping mat in her quarters.

After Adia was gone, E'ranale appeared next to her daughter. "I consider it progress that she did not question how you are here, yet are also to come to Kthama."

"Perhaps understanding is dawning, that the true part of each of us exists here in eternity—even as we experience existence in the time-bound realm."

"Pan," said E'ranale quietly, "we must pray that Adia's faith in the Order of Function will be strong enough to carry her through what is to come."

"I know," Pan said with a heavy sigh.

## CHAPTER 4

Haan and Haaka were sitting in the Great Chamber at Kht'shWea. Also, there were Sastak, Dorn, Ar-Rak, who was one of Dorn's guards, Qirrik, whom Haan had appointed High Protector, and the Healer, Artadel. Kalli was playing on the rock floor at Haaka's feet.

The memories of Tarnor and the Sassen rebels' intent to take over Kthama had faded. With the former leader, Tarnor, killed by the Straf'Tor, under Dorn's influence, the rebel Sassen had seamlessly blended in with Haan's group.

"As you know, Acaraho, who was the High Protector, is now the Leader of Kthama. I assure you this change will have no negative effect on our relationship. Though I grieve the loss to us of Khon'Tor's daily wisdom and guidance, I have complete faith in Acaraho's goodwill toward us."

Dorn spoke. "My group and I are very apprecia-tive of your accepting us here, Adik'Tar. Never have we experienced so rich a life as we have now. Our females are relieved of much toil in having the Mother Stream below, and the moisture takes the spark out of the air, which often troubled us at Kayerm."

"At Kthama," said Haan, "the High Protector and the primary female organizer work together to coor-dinate projects, tasks, and assignments, including harvesting. As the cold weather draws closer, we will be busy gathering supplies to weather-over. We must be aware of not raiding the Akassa areas. We consume much more than they do, and we must not disadvantage them in any way, nor abuse their generosity in giving us Kht'shWea."

Haan continued, "I will meet with Acaraho and ask him to direct us to areas which they are not using or not planning to use. Also, perhaps we should offer to gift a portion of our harvest to them every season from now on, as an expression of our thanks."

All the others nodded.

"It will be a relief to get a break from this heat," said Sastak. "I doubt the Akassa appreciate the cold weather as we do. Perhaps we can be of service to them when the harsh winter storms come. After all, Straf'Tor commanded us to care for and protect them."

Kalli was happily entertaining herself, and Haaka

looked up from watching her daughter. "Where are Thord and Lellaach?" Do you not wish them to be part of these meetings?"

"Thord came to me and said the twelve Guardians would disappear on and off for long periods. He assured me there was nothing to be concerned about, but that they need to meet separately from us," explained Haan.

"Does that not concern you?" asked Dorn.

"Perhaps, if I did not know them all as I do. But they have a different destiny now that they are Guardians. I trust that Thord will explain it to me in due time."

"I mean no disrespect to Kalli," said Dorn as he nodded to the offling playing on the floor. "But is this our future?"

Kalli looked up when she heard her name.

Haan sighed. Haaka frowned at Dorn, who caught her expression.

"I apologize, Haaka. I realize that remark sounded critical," he stammered.

Haaka reached down and picked up Kalli. "Is this so bad if it *is* our future?" she asked, holding Kalli up on her knee. "Yes, she looks more Akassa than Sassen. But what does that matter? She is a sweet soul; she is an offling and deserves our love and protection no matter what she looks like. If we have to breed with the Akassa to survive, at least we *will* survive."

Dorn briefly looked up to the ceiling as if praying for a way to correct his blunder.

"Again, I apologize. But we need to discuss our future now that we are settling into a routine. We carry what is left of the Mothoc blood. If it is diluted even further, where does that leave Etera? Was that not the purpose of the Rah'hora? To keep our blood-line separate from that of the Akassa?"

"I do not know the answer, Dorn," said Haan. "It is true that crossing with the Akassa would further dilute the Mothoc blood. But if it is that or disappear entirely, what choice do we have? Perhaps if we can increase our population, the numbers will compensate for the loss in concentration. I can only trust that, hidden from our awareness, the Order of Functions is working this out as always."

"The Order of Functions. If there is no Guardian to connect with the Aezaiterian field, nor the Order of Functions, how can we believe things are unfolding as they should be?"

"I do not know; I only have faith that they are. We did not know how we would open Kht'shWea. When I consider the path that brought us to where we are now, living in a place just as resplendent as Kthama, I cannot help but believe we have been guided. We have been given twelve Guardians, transformed by the life force released when we opened Kht'shWea. And An'Kru, the Promised One, has come. As for Guardians, Pan was the last of the Mothoc Guardians, and since they are virtually immortal, it is likely that somewhere she still walks Etera."

The group fell silent; the thought that Pan could still be alive immediately filled them with a sense of awe and hope.

○

In the Healer's Quarters at the Far High Hills, Urilla Wuti sat across from her niece, Iella. "We must restart your lessons in earnest. You have progressed much on your own, but I want to meet regularly from now on."

Iella was gazing off across the room, and Urilla Wuti cocked her head, "Are you listening to me?"

Iella turned her attention back to her aunt. "I am sorry. I am a bit distracted."

"I know. So this is a good time for us to continue your training; you will not always have the luxury of peace of mind in which to work."

Urilla Wuti reached out to take Iella's hands and opened a Connection with her. When, after some time, they separated, Urilla Wuti said, "Do you wish to talk about it?"

"There is nothing to say," Iella laughed. "You now know everything."

"I know about the situation, how you feel, what you have experienced, but I do not know what you will decide to do about it."

"I do not know what to do about it. My place is

here. Nootau's place is at the High Rocks. There seems to be no solution. Yet I cannot get him out of my mind, or my heart," Iella covered her face with her hands and slumped forward.

Urilla Wuti leaned over and put her arm around the young Healer's shoulders.

"It is best you forget about Nootau'Tor. As you said, your duty is here. And even though the High Rocks is only several days' trip away, it would be too difficult to split your time between two places, especially being a Healer. You are young; there will be someone else."

Iella lifted her head and broke from Urilla Wuti's embrace. "How can you say that?" She stood up and began pacing. "How can you tell me to forget about Nootau? Have you never been in love? There will not ever be another like him. He is kind and generous, and just seeing him makes my heart sing. *Find someone else*? And live the rest of my life longing for one male, yet bonded to another? I cannot bear even the thought of it."

"Then you have your answer," Urilla Wuti said.

"What?"

"If that is how you truly feel, and if he feels the same about you, find a way to make it work. Make a way for it to work."

"Did you just trick me?"

"No. I only showed you your own fears and doubts and gave you an opportunity to bring them into the open."

Iella laughed with relief, "Will I ever be as wise as you?" she asked.

"There is no answer I can give that does not ultimately flatter myself," Urilla Wuti said and smiled. "That being a given, the answer is yes, of course you will be."

"I have been avoiding him, and he knows it. And I know it hurts him." Iella's voice had dropped from the lilting happiness of a moment ago. "I hope he has not left."

"If he cares for you as you care for him, I doubt you could run him off that easily.

"But," added Urilla Wuti, "not even our lessons can compete with true love, so go find him if you must. We can practice later this afternoon."

With that, Iella leaned over, hugged her aunt briefly, and practically flew out of the door.

And ran smack into Thorak.

"Wait, wait, what is the hurry?" he said as he grabbed her by the shoulders spinning her around to face him.

"Stop, let me go; I have something I must do," she looked down at his hands wrapped tight around her upper arms. She shrugged, trying to loosen his grip.

"You are hurting me," she said

Just then, having heard the commotion, Urilla Wuti came out of the Healer's Quarters.

"Let her go, Thorak." Urilla Wuti narrowed her eyes and stepped toward the male who was three times her size.

"Va!" Thorak said, releasing his grasp on Iella. She rubbed her arms where the imprints from the pressure of his grasp had reddened. "Go then; find your precious Nootau. But this is not over," and he stormed off.

Iella turned to the older Healer, who drew her into a motherly embrace.

"What has happened to him? If Harak'Sar finds out how he is behaving, he may lose his post as High Protector. A person of his authority cannot act this way," Iella said.

"Desire can be pleasurable when the object of our longing is within reach. But otherwise, it can become a cruel master."

"I still need to find Nootau," Iella said.

"Come, we will look for him together."

❦

Nootau was nowhere to be found, raising Iella's fears that he had left Far High Hills and returned to Kthama. Finally, they ran into Dreth, who said Nootau was out assisting in gathering the late summer crops with the offspring and Urilla Wuti's Helper, Hollia. Together, Urilla Wuti and Iella walked the path down to the planting area, easily spotting Nootau, who towered over the offspring he was working with.

As they approached, they could hear laughter and giggles coming from the youngest ones and saw that flowers were being tossed back and forth in a mock battle. Iella smiled as Nootau pretended to be felled by an onslaught of blossoms and gracefully crumpled to the ground as if having succumbed to the attack. Riotous laughter broke out among his assailants.

"I swear, Nootau," said Hollia, pretending to scold him, "You are as bad as the offspring. Let us get on with it, or we will not be done by darkfall."

To the delight of the offspring, who continued to laugh at his antics, Nootau dragged himself back to life. As he rose and was brushing himself off, he glanced over to see Urilla Wuti and Iella watching him. A huge smile broke across his face.

Iella waded through the tall plants to meet him. "For a moment there, I thought you were done for. I am glad to see you survived the attack." She glanced over at the offspring, who were avidly watching the two adults approach each other.

"I put up my best fight, but they beat me anyway," he said, pretending to scowl at them, which caused them to laugh again even harder.

Hollia came over and shooed the offspring away and back to work, though, as they were walking off, they turned their heads to watch.

"You have not been to evening meal for some time," said Nootau. "I was worried about you."

"I needed some time to myself," she said. "I have had a lot on my mind."

"I see," he said.

"I heard what you told me, about having to protect An'Kru, about being there for him, and I did not want to cause you complications. That is why I stayed away."

"Did you think staying away would change my feelings for you?"

"I guess."

"Have they changed yours for me?" he asked, searching her eyes.

"Only to make them stronger. I realize I do not want to be with anyone but you. I do not know how to work it out, but I know I cannot turn away from how I feel," Iella said.

Nootau exhaled deeply. He took her hands in his. "We will find a way, Saraste'." He leaned down, gently drew her to him, and pressed his lips against hers. He stopped suddenly as squeals of delight rose from the group of offspring who, against Hollia's orders, had paused to watch the love story unfolding in front of them. Even Hollia was smiling.

Then Nootau picked Iella up, gently hoisted her over his shoulder, and started to walk away, calling over to his fellow harvesters, "We have to go now. I will rejoin you tomorrow." They all giggled, and Iella, still bundled over his shoulder, laughed the hardest of them all.

A few feet away, he put her down. "Sorry about that," he smiled. "I got a little carried away," and he helped her smooth her ruffled hair back into place.

"I am happier than I ever imagined I could be," she said. "But what will become of us?"

"Whatever we decide," Nootau said. Turning to Urilla Wuti, he asked, "How do we get hold of the Overseer to find out when the next pairing ceremony will be?"

Urilla Wuti smiled, "You are looking at her."

A frown creased Nootau's brow.

"No," he said. "I mean Kurak'Kahn, the Overseer."

"Kurak'Kahn is no longer Overseer of the High Council. I am," she smiled, enjoying the moment. "At least, temporarily."

"I do not know how that happened, but I am sure someone will explain it to me in time. I cannot imagine a better choice; congratulations."

Urilla Wuti smiled, "At the next High Council meeting, I will let the others know that there has been a request for a pairing. From what I know of your bloodlines, I am confident there will be no issue."

Nootau looked away for a fleeting moment. "I must tell my parents." He looked back at Iella. "What of your mother? Thorak said she favored him for your mate."

"She did until she met you. Do you not remember how she was fawning over you at your first meeting? She was practically throwing me at you," she laughed. "I suspect she will be thrilled."

Drista was indeed thrilled. Iella, Urilla Wuti, and

Nootau found her in the eating area, chatting with several other females. She looked over as she saw them approaching, and a big smile crossed her face.

"I am glad to see you two together; what have you been up to?" she asked as they reached her. Belatedly, she greeted Urilla Wuti.

"Mother," started Iella. "Please do not overreact. But Nootau and I are going to ask to be paired."

Drista jumped up from her seat and threw her arms around her daughter, who rolled her eyes.

"Is this handsome fellow the lucky one?" one of the friends asked.

Drista turned to them, taking Nootau by the arm. He glanced back at Iella and smiled as her mother dragged him closer to the others.

"This is Nootau'Tor; he is the son of the new Leader of the High Rocks, Acaraho'Tor. He and my daughter recently got acquainted when he came to study with her and Urilla Wuti."

"A male with an interest in healing?" another asked.

"Well, I am interested in learning, but there was also another reason," he smiled, and he looked back at Iella and winked. The females chittered gleefully among themselves.

Then reality hit her, and with concern, Drista asked, "Where will you live? Nootau, are you planning on coming to the Far High Hills? I know it is the norm for the female to go to the male's community, but Iella has a calling here."

"Mother," interrupted Iella, "we have not worked out those details. But we will."

"Everything in me says that this union is meant to be. Celebrate the joy, and the rest will work itself out," advised Urilla Wuti.

The others all nodded, though one of Drista's friends leaned over, her face pinched. "But, Drista, what of Thorak? I thought you favored a union for your daughter with him."

"Thorak has adored Iella all her life. He would have protected her, and she would have had a good position here, not only as a Healer but also as mate of the High Protector. He would have been a good provider. But this one, his heart is deeply genuine. The minute I met him I knew they should be together."

"I have seen how Thorak looks at Iella. I do not see him taking it well," the friend commented.

The others nodded and exchanged concerned glances.

They were right. Word reached Thorak quickly, and no, he was not taking it well.

The High Protector stormed through the tunnels of Amara, looking for Nootau. Not finding his rival there, he started searching outside. He found Nootau speaking with a group of other males about the same age, all talking in animated voices, full of high spirits.

They saw Thorak bounding toward them and relaxed the circle, standing aside to watch. They could tell he had his sights on Nootau and guessed what it was about.

"Slow down, Thorak," said one of them, stepping forward.

"Get out of my way if you know what is good for you," and Thorak forced his way past. As he got to Nootau, he drew back to throw a punch. Nootau swung his arm up, catching Thorak's forearm and deflecting the blow. He then grabbed Thorak's arm, twisting it back and holding his opponent in a chokehold.

Thorak struggled violently to escape, but Nootau used his right leg to sweep Thorak's feet out from under him, and the High Protector thudded to the ground, sending dust flying.

Nootau immediately dropped full body onto Thorak, rolling him face down, and with one knee, pinned the High Protector in place.

"Enough. Enough, Thorak," he shouted. "This is not going to solve anything. The female has the right of choice and refusal. It is dishonorable to continue attacking me. She did not want you even before I came; you need to accept it and move on with your life."

Thorak continued to struggle, and Nootau kept his position, waiting for the rejected suitor to exhaust himself.

"For what it is worth, I am sorry. But if not me, it

would have been someone else. The heart cannot be controlled. We cannot help who we love."

"Listen to Nootau," one of the others called out. "He is telling you the truth. We all feel bad for you, but it is not Nootau's fault. It is no one's fault."

Thorak finally stopped struggling. "Let me up," he said.

"I do not wish to fight you, Thorak. But if you continue, I will. And we will both suffer for it. Eventually, if you keep this up, it will only turn Iella's feelings against you. And word will get out. In the end, you will only dishonor yourself."

Nootau eased the pressure off his rival and extended a hand to help him up, but Thorak slapped it away.

"There are many females who would rush at the chance to be paired with you, I am sure," Nootau said. "You can probably have any other female you want."

"I do not need your sympathy," Thorak barked as he brushed off the soil that clung to him. "And I do not want any other female. I want Iella. You have stolen what was rightfully mine. I suggest you leave now, while you still can," and he snarled, fully exposing his canines, before stomping off.

"He is not going to let it go, is he?" Nootau said to no one in particular as he watched Thorak retreat.

"No, he is not. Eventually, Harak'Sar will get word of this, and it will not go well for Thorak," said one of the males standing there.

Indeed, it did not take long for word to reach Harak'Sar.

The Leader of the Far High Hills stood waiting for Thorak. At his side were the First Guard, Dreth, and the Overseer, Urilla Wuti.

When he saw the three together, Thorak knew immediately what he had been called there for.

"I imagine you know what this is about," began Harak'Sar.

Thorak lifted his chin and said, "It is about the pairing of Nootau'Tor of the High Rocks and Iella Onida of the Far High Hills."

"No. It is about your actions regarding their intended pairing. I have heard reports that you have repeatedly confronted Nootau, and more seriously, physically accosted Iella."

Thorak narrowed his eyes at Urilla Wuti, the only other who knew he had grabbed Iella in the hallway outside the Healer's Quarters.

Harak'Sar caught the expression and stepped forward, his face inches from Thorak's. "That will be enough," he said. "I have always trusted you, depended on you. But this aggression toward others has given me great pause. Every male here can understand the pain of losing a favored female. There is compassion for your situation, but there will be no tolerance for your actions—at least not from us. You have always conducted yourself without reproach. Your behavior over this is difficult to reconcile with who I know you to be.

"For the immediate future, your duties as High Protector are suspended. Dreth will pick up the extra load. I suggest you take this time to reflect on what you are doing to your life and your reputation. Nothing you can do will change the fact that these two are in love and *will* be paired. Your focus now needs to be on how to repair your good standing in my eyes and in those of the watchers and guards."

Thorak now turned his glare to Harak'Sar. "So everyone knows about this?"

"What did you expect? You have publicly confronted both Iella and Nootau. And because of your station, you are doubly accountable for your actions." Harak'Sar let out a long breath. "Now go to your quarters until evening meal. If I hear again of you aggressively approaching either Iella or Nootau, there will be further consequences."

*You say you understand, but do you? If you felt the same way as I did about a female as I do her, you would not think it so easy to simply move on.* But Thorak bowed slightly and left as the others watched him go.

"Do you think he took you seriously?" asked Urilla Wuti.

"Based on the look in his eyes, I would say no," Harak'Sar said. "I fear this is not going to end well for him."

He continued, "Dreth, pass the word among your

males. Have whoever is around Thorak to keep an eye on him. Better yet, see if you can find someone to follow him unobtrusively when he leaves his quarters. I hate to be duplicitous, but I suspect this is not over by any means.

"And now that Thorak has left, please find Nootau and bring him here."

Before too long, Nootau was standing before Harak'Sar.

"Adik'Tar 'Sar," Nootau said, nodding to the Leader. "You wished to speak with me?"

"I have heard word of Thorak's actions toward you and Iella. I want you to know that this is not at all like Thorak. He has observed his position with honor, and until now, behaved admirably. Until now."

"I understand he is heartbroken, and I am sorry for his suffering."

Harak'Sar looked at Nootau, "You have a good heart. Much like your father. Most males in your situation would have no compassion for their adversary. But a word of advice; keep your distance from Thorak until things cool down. I would not have thought him capable of what he has already done, so I cannot predict how far out of line his feelings may drive him."

"Harak'Sar is right," said Urilla Wuti. "Do not

drop your guard. Thorak is clearly deeply disturbed by this and definitely not in control of his emotions. Perhaps time will allow his wounds to heal, and he will come back to his senses. But from the anger I sense vehemently raging inside him, I am not hopeful."

# CHAPTER 5

Akar'Tor was miserable. It was a miracle he had survived this long on his own. He had left Kayerm and traveled south, away from the People's communities, eventually joining the Great River and following her banks. He was surviving on fish he speared in the shallows and whatever roots and berries he could find. He did not know his destination, only that after what he had witnessed during the Sarnonn rebel attack, he needed to get safely away from Kthama. His heart became harder with each step of his journey.

After many days' travel, he spotted what looked like a small cave. It was situated a short distance up the hillside, close enough to the Great River, but not too close. He approached it carefully, prepared to meet any occupants. He gingerly entered, waiting for his eyes to adjust, his hearing alert for any sound of movement—the snap of a twig or a scuffle of dirt.

After a few moments of silence, he could see well enough. Searching for prints, he found what could only belong to one of the People. He went a little farther in, past the first chamber and down a short tunnel, anxiety rising at the thought of being trapped. In the next chamber, he found crude woven baskets, hollowed-out gourds, and leftover nut casings, clearing all doubt that the caves were occupied—or had recently been. *Who?* he asked himself. A moment later, strong hands grabbed him by the shoulders and spun him around.

"What are you doing here?" shouted a male voice, just before everything went black.

Akar'Tor woke to a raging headache. He rolled over and levered himself up on one elbow, shaking his head to clear it, as with his other hand, he touched the lump on the back of his head. A male he did not recognize was squatting in the corner, watching him.

"Who are you?" Akar'Tor asked, "And why did you attack me?"

"The better question would be, who are you? But I already know the answer to that. You are Akar'Tor, Khon'Tor's son. I thought you were Khon'Tor, and that is why I hit you on the head with that rock," he said, pointing at it. "You are lucky I did not kill you. If you had been Khon'Tor, believe me, I would have, though, of course, only after a satisfyingly prolonged period of torture."

"Well, whoever you are, we share the same enemy," Akar'Tor said, moving carefully into an upright position.

"I am Kahrok. Khon'Tor banished me from the High Rocks, just as he did you, and I have been living here since I was expelled. That is if you call this in any way *living*—"

"What did you do?"

"I told them I had seen you with the rebel Sarnonn."

"You were banished for that? Seems that they would have valued that information."

"I made the mistake of telling Khon'Tor in front of his precious mate, Tehya. The news upset her so much that she threw up. For that, I was banished."

*Tehya.* "Still seems excessive," Akar'Tor said.

"The High Protector, Acaraho, sent word to the other communities with instructions that I ask one of them for asylum—that they would accept me on the condition that I was never again in the presence of Khon'Tor or his mate. Should they visit that community, I would need to vacate it until they left. But I had my own ideas, so I started heading south instead."

"It is a hard life, living alone. I know. Why would you not take up Acaraho on his offer?"

"I am not done with Khon'Tor. Whatever the

consequences, I am going to settle my score with him one way or another," said Kahrok.

"I have my own score to settle with him," said Akar'Tor.

"Well, whatever your intentions, you had better get to your father first. I plan on killing him."

"You can have that pleasure. There is only one thing I want now, and that is his mate, Tehya. Perhaps we can work together?"

Kahrok thought for a moment. "Alright."

"Good, give me a few days to come up with a plan," said Akar'Tor.

Larara and Kurak'Kahn had returned to their community and tried to resume their lives. Their offspring kept a close watch over them, sharing in their grief over the loss of Linoi and her offspring. No one had seen any sign of Berak, nor had U'Kail's little body been recovered. The mystery was weighing heavily on both of them. If they could only know what had taken place after Berak left with the offspring.

Berak sat huddled under a small bit of brush he had assembled into a makeshift shelter. His mind had drifted to his last encounter with Linoi, and he was feeling uncomfortable.

*I should not have argued with her so. I should never have lost my temper and struck her. And to have taken U'Kail; that was a vile act, and besides it being a great deal of trouble having to look after him. No doubt I will suffer in krell for what I have done. Perhaps I can still find the offspring alive where I left him. I have to try. It has not been long.*

Berak jumped up and set off to where he had left U'Kail. He searched the area, trying to remember the exact place. He had abandoned the offspring close to where there was a village of the Brothers, hoping that he might be found. In his twisted thinking at the time, Berak had persuaded himself that whatever happened afterward was fate—that he had not directly harmed U'Kail.

There was no sign of the offspring or of his body. Berak continued looking around closely and finally found a set of tracks leading to and away from where he might have abandoned U'Kail. *Could it be that someone saw me leave him? Or, later, heard him crying and found him?*

The tracks were small and close together, and Berak followed them until they ended at a mere trickle of a stream. *The prints are too small to be made by an adult of the People. They could belong either to an adolescent, but that's unlikely so far away. One of the Brothers? Maybe one of them did find him. And if they did*

*and they take him to one of our communities, I will be
long gone, so I am safe.*

For a brief moment, Berak thought of crossing
the stream and continuing to look for U'Kail. *No.
That will prove my guilt. At least I can believe he is alive
somewhere. If whoever found him had meant him ill will,
they would most likely have dispatched him then and
there. At least I tried. Now I will head west to the community of the Far Flats. Surely word will not have traveled
that far. They have not participated in any of the Ashwea
Awhidis or community events—not for decades. They
will wonder why I have left my community, but I have
time to make up a plausible story, as it will take me a long
time to get there, anyway. Many years ago, my mother's
sister was paired with someone from there; perhaps I can
build on that as my reason.*

Berak returned to his makeshift shelter and
started to prepare for the long journey.

Young Myrica was out foraging hazelnuts and acorns
when she heard someone walking not too far from
her. She was alone, so she ducked and hid in the
nearby bushes. Through the thick cover, she could
see well enough to spot a large muscular form and
recognized it as one of the People, a male. He was
carrying something in his arms. She held her breath
as he passed close by, grateful that she was down
wind, and he would not catch her scent.

She watched as the male set down what he was carrying, something that appeared to be moving. Then she heard a small sound and her heart caught. She clasped both her hands over her mouth, hard, to stifle a cry.

It was a baby. *What is a male doing all the way out here with a child?*

She continued to watch as he stood there for a few moments. It was all Myrica could do not to cry out. *I am powerless against a male of his size. But what am I to do? I cannot stand here and let him harm that child.* Against her better judgment, Myrica was about to get up and confront whoever it was, but she saw him slowly turn and walk away. He was not going to kill it; he was just going to leave it. She gradually, silently, let out her breath, but she feared he would hear her heart pounding. The child sat where he had been left and watched the male leave.

It felt like an eternity before Myrica felt it safe to come out. She could hear the baby playing quietly but knew that before long, something would cause it to cry, quickly attracting predators.

She crept out of her cover and looked around before quickly walking over. It looked at her, studying her face for a moment. She gently scooped it up, along with the hide that had been left with it. She carefully made her escape and traveled down a small incline, across the stream toward her village, moving as fast and as silently as possible.

No one noticed Myrica until she approached a

group of females working on sorting a harvest of various fruits and vegetables. The medicine woman, Tiponi, looked up, and realizing Myrica was carrying something that could only be a child, trotted over to her.

"What have you got?" she asked.

"It is one of the People's children. I was out gathering hazelnuts and acorns, and I heard one of their males coming from up the incline below. I hid in the bushes and watched as he abandoned the child." She explained how afraid she had been that the baby would be harmed and how, after the male had left, she went and collected it.

"There is no way of knowing which community it came from," said Tiponi. "Both are equidistant from us."

"He is a male, and we cannot return him. What if the male who abandoned him finds out? What is to keep him from doing the same again—or worse? We have not had contact with the People in a very long time. What do we really know about them?"

Tiponi thought for a moment. "I will seek the counsel of Chief Kotori. But for now, I agree with you."

"I'm sure he will be hungry soon."

"Wait in your shelter; I will find Alvoa and send her to you; she has little ones and will have food for him. And then I will speak with Chief Kotori."

Myrica went to her shelter and sat down with the child. She smoothed back his dark hair and looked into his eyes. "I will do my best by you, little one. I pray you have a gentle spirit and will learn to harness your greater strength, lest as you grow, you must be isolated from the other children your age. Now, what to name you?"

Myrica sat thinking of names and playing with the child, who was able to walk, slightly unsteadily. When Alvoa arrived, she helped the young mother to feed him.

Tiponi found Chief Kotori and Second Chief Tawa discussing winter preparations in the Chief's shelter.

Chief Kotori signaled for her to enter.

"Myrica has returned from foraging. She discovered an abandoned child."

They looked up but said nothing, waiting for her to tell them more.

"Alvoa is helping Myrica care for him. He is one of the People."

"How did it come to be out here, so far from any of their communities?"

"He was abandoned by one of their males. Myrica saw it all."

The two Chiefs nodded slowly.

"She fears for his safety if we return him to one of their communities. Not knowing where he came from, or if whoever left him would discover he had been returned, and perhaps, the second time, do him more direct harm. Since we do not have an active relationship with the People, she feels we cannot know which of them to trust."

"Is she prepared to take responsibility for it? Or should we find a family, perhaps?" asked Second Chief Tawa.

"At this moment, I think she wishes to claim him and raise him as her own."

"Even if it is addled or unhealthy, I believe it cannot be the way of the People—to abandon one of their own. This must have been a rogue act. Since we cannot know right away, we will keep it among us for now. Perhaps, in time, we will learn whose it is and why it was abandoned. Remind Myrica that the child does not belong to us. She must be prepared to surrender it back to its people once we determine if that can be done safely."

"I will let Myrica know of your decision. Thank you." Tiponi bowed her head and left to find Myrica.

Several days after encountering Akar'Tor, Kahrok set out for the Overseer's community, which was known to have fewer guards than the other locations. Being the highest authority, the Overseer's word would carry the credibility needed to summon Khon'Tor. He took nothing with him except the plan he and Akar'Tor had come up with. He went over and over it in his mind as he followed the Great River down toward his destination. As he approached, the few watchers positioned there sent word that someone was coming

Kurak'Kahn was notified and came to meet the guest. Larara went with him, as they had been sitting together at the morning meal when the word came.

Kurak'Kahn stood with his guards by his side as a tall scruffy-looking male entered.

"Who are you, and why have you come?" he asked.

"I have come to tell you to send word to Khon'Tor that I know the whereabouts of his son, Akar'Tor, who he has been looking for. He will want to know this, I assure you."

"You have not told me who you are."

"It does not matter who I am, only that I can lead Khon'Tor to his estranged son," said Kahrok.

"I do not know where you can find Khon'Tor, nor do I care about him or any of his troubles. Best you be on your way; I am finished with anything to do with High Rocks," and the former Overseer stalked off. He called back to the guards, "Make sure he leaves promptly."

Kahrok stood with his mouth open. *We had not counted on this,* he thought.

Then the female turned to him. "Please excuse my mate. We have been suffering through difficult times for a while now. Khon'Tor is at the Far High Hills. You can find him there."

It did not take long for the watchers at the Far High Hills to alert Harak'Sar that a stranger was approaching.

First Guard Dreth met the burly stranger at the entrance.

"I have come to see Khon'Tor."

"What do you want with him?" Dreth asked, buying time for Harak'Sar to get there.

"I have information of interest to him, trust me."

Harak'Sar arrived shortly, accompanied by Urilla Wuti.

"What is this about?" the Leader asked, looking the unkempt male up and down. It was obvious he had been on his own for some time. "Who are you, and what do you want?"

"I have come to make amends with Khon'Tor. He will want to know what I have to tell him. It is about his son, Akar'Tor."

Urilla Wuti looked at Harak'Sar and nodded.

"Go and find Khon'Tor, quickly," Harak'Sar said. He had sized up the visitor and realized that in such a weakened state, the young male posed no threat.

Dreth returned with Khon'Tor, who had to exercise all his self-control not to lunge out when he saw who was standing there.

"Why are you here? I told you to stay away from anywhere near Tehya." He held Kahrok with an icy glare.

"I remember." Kahrok eyed his enemy. "But I

know Akar'Tor's whereabouts. I can take you to him."

"Tell me where he is instead, then you can go on your way," snarled Khon'Tor.

"You will need me to guide you, or you will never find him in time, trust me. Even now, I cannot guarantee he is still there."

"Why have you come to tell me this?"

"I wish to make amends, to ask your forgiveness."

Khon'Tor eyed the male suspiciously. *I do not trust him, but I have no choice; this is the only lead anyone has given me about Akar's whereabouts.* "Give me a few moments to consider your offer," he said.

"Every moment you delay is another moment he could be on his way elsewhere."

*It is a trap. I can feel it. Yet what choice do I have but to go? No doubt he knows where Akar is. And now that he knows where Tehya is, it means Akar will soon know if he doesn't already. At least I can see this attack coming and be prepared for it.*

Khon'Tor turned to Harak'Sar and Urilla Wuti, "I must go. Urilla Wuti, I claim First Law," he said, as he was no longer in a position of authority and had no jurisdiction to dispatch those who threatened others.

Urilla Wuti replied, "My term may be the shortest ever as Overseer, but you have my backing to protect yourself and your loved ones. I will defend you and stand with you if it comes to that."

"Do not try following," said Kahrok to Harak'Sar. "I feel I can confidently take the two of us to where he is hiding, but not with a troop warning him of our approach."

Khon'Tor thought of the weapon he had made just for this opportunity. It was still at the High Rocks with High Protector Awan. The Waschini blade was also out of reach, tucked high up in the cubby hole in his quarters.

"I need to say goodbye to my mate," Khon'Tor said, thinking of retrieving the blade.

Kahrok scoffed, "I can see you do not believe me. No matter. No loss to me. Find him on your own then," and Kahrok turned to leave.

*Quat!* "Wait, I am coming with you," Khon'Tor said. He was in far better shape than Kahrok, so it was a risk he was prepared to take.

"I will let Tehya know you have had to leave," said Urilla Wuti. "There is no way we cannot tell her."

Khon'Tor turned to Kahrok. "Lead the way." And together, the two males walked from the Far High Hills.

❂

Urilla Wuti made the long walk to the quarters of Khon'Tor and Tehya, realizing that Tehya was no doubt busy caring for Arismae. She announced herself outside the door, and a voice called out for her to enter.

Tehya looked up from playing with Arismae, who

sat on her lap, and greeted Urilla Wuti. "It is always good to see you," she said happily.

Urilla Wuti sighed. "A visitor came here a few moments ago. It was Kahrok, whom your mate banished from the High Rocks some time ago."

'The one who brought news of Akar'Tor? Khon'Tor practically beat him to a pulp over that."

"Yes. He came to tell Khon'Tor that he knows of Akar'Tor's whereabouts."

Tehya's eyes grew wide. "*Where is Khon'Tor now?*"

"He left with Kahrok."

"On his own?"

"I am afraid so; those were the terms."

"No, no, it must be a trap; I can feel it. Oh, Urila Wuti, no. Without a doubt, the two are working together. *They will kill him*. He had to know it was a trap!"

"I am sure he did. But he was not about to lose the chance to settle things with Akar'Tor. No matter how the odds are stacked against him. Until someone stops him, Akar'Tor will always be trying to get to you. I understand why Khon'Tor would not let this opportunity pass. Remember, the greatest enemy is the one you do not see coming. He knows what he is probably walking into. Next time, he might not be forewarned."

Tehya cuddled Arismae close and began rocking her back and forth. *I cannot lose him. This cannot be happening. Oh, why, Great Spirit, is this not already over, once and for all.* "Did anyone follow them?"

"We were warned not to," said Urilla Wuti. "And I know Khon'Tor, he would not want us to do anything to jeopardize his finding Akar'Tor.

"I will be back with something to calm you. You are right; most likely, Akar and Kahrok are working together. But Khon'Tor is smart; he will have figured that out. Now, promise me you will stay here. There is nothing you can do except, with us all, to pray for his protection."

A while later, Urilla Wuti came back with Iella and something to calm Tehya's nerves. After the Healers had left, Tehya set the drink aside. She did not need to calm down; what she needed to do now was *think*.

Khon'Tor followed behind Kahrok, his senses alert. They walked for some time, only stopping for short rests. As they walked, Khon'Tor studied Kahrok, noting the tone of his muscles, the length of his stride, and sizing up how depleted the young male was from living on his own. Khon'Tor tried to think ahead to where they might be going. For now, they were following the banks of the Great River. He had never been this far and did not know what lay ahead other than perhaps more of the same terrain. If they veered from the riverbank, he would note any feature that might serve as a landmark for when he returned.

"How much farther?" Khon'Tor asked.

"Not very much, if he is still where I saw him."

*Where you left him, you mean*, thought Khon'Tor.

Having spent the last few days gathering what they needed to carry out the plan, Akar'Tor sat alone in the small cave. Now that everything was arranged, there was nothing to do but wait. He passed the time entertaining fantasies of what he wanted to do to his father—and Tehya.

Kahrok glanced back at Khon'Tor. "Why do you wear that wrap around your shoulders? Is it not hot and uncomfortable?"

"It is of no matter to you. Shut up and keep walking," Khon'Tor said, picking his way through the rocky terrain.

"I can tell that you do not trust me. Please, believe me, I only want to make up for the pain I caused your mate by telling you about Akar'Tor in front of her."

"Do not think for a moment that I do not know this is a trap, Kahrok. So do not dishonor yourself further with your lies," Khon'Tor snapped.

"Soon enough, you will see how wrong you are," Kahrok answered. "And you will be thanking me.

You might never have another opportunity like this."

They continued on, following the Great River. In time, Khon'Tor became aware of a distant, small opening in the rocks that lined a large incline. He followed the turn of Kahrok's head and realized they were looking at the same place. *That must be our destination.*

As they approached the opening, Kahrok stepped aside. "The last time I saw him, he was in there." Kahrok motioned for Khon'Tor to enter.

However, Khon'Tor stood back. "You go first."

Kahrok shrugged and ducked under the low rocks above the entrance.

Khon'Tor followed him, every nerve on end. Once inside, he stopped to let his low-light vision catch up. It was a small entrance with a short tunnel leading off it. He could see that the tunnel opened into a larger chamber not far ahead.

Kahrok entered cautiously, calling for Khon'Tor to follow him. Then the young male stepped a few feet into the chamber before turning back. "We are too late; he has already left."

As Khon'Tor entered the chamber, Akar'Tor stepped out behind him, and with a rock, smashed his father on the back of the head.

Khon'Tor spat dust out of his mouth and tried to blink it out of his eyes. He shook his head in an attempt to clear his thoughts. He was lying on his side, his arms secured behind him. His feet were also tightly tied at the ankles. He quickly glanced around the cave, getting his bearings, and saw Kahrok and Akar'Tor in a corner. He closed his eyes and feigned unconsciousness.

When Kahrok had called out that they were too late, Khon'Tor realized it was a signal and prepared himself for some type of attack. There had been a lot of time to picture the many ways in which the two youngsters would try to overpower him. As he and Kahrok had approached the cave, he narrowed it down to some type of blow, either with a rock or a heavy branch. Since he was convinced that his capture was somehow part of a ploy ultimately to get to Tehya, he was also confident they would not kill him. At least not right away.

"Remember, I get Khon'Tor," said Kahrok. "And you get Tehya."

"Whether he dies at your hand or mine does not matter to me. As long as he first gets to watch me with his precious mate, taking my time to do every filthy thing I can think of while he listens helplessly as she screams for him to save her. And when I am done with Tehya, you can take a turn."

Akar'Tor's hatred was tangible.

Khon'Tor felt his heart almost burst even as his blood ran cold.

# CHAPTER 6

Acaraho, Adia, and Oh'Dar set out for the Far High Hills to meet with the High Council members and Urilla Wuti. After receiving acknowledgment from the new Overseer, and word that Risik'Tar of the Great Pines and Lesharo'Mok of the Deep Valley were traveling back, Acaraho had sent word ahead that they were also on their way. He explained that their pace would be a little slower because of Oh'Dar. Paytah'Tar of the High Red Rocks had sent word that he would not be coming, and they had received no response from the Little River, which was not unusual for the distant, reclusive community.

Adia had placed An'Kru securely in a sling, stopping to nurse him and clean him up as needed along the way. Oh'Dar carried a hide satchel slung over his shoulder in which he had brought dried treats for Kweeuu.

"I will be glad to see Nootau," Oh'Dar said as they stopped to rest.

"I wonder how he and Iella are getting along." Adia smiled, "When Nootau was there with us after An'Kru was born, he started a friendship with Urilla Wuti's niece Iella. It may have blossomed into something more."

"I would be happy for him if that were true," said Oh'Dar. "Though I would hate to see him in the same position as I am, torn between two communities with a mate in one and you and Father in another."

"You have three communities to worry about, actually," his mother reminded him. "It is the pull to Shadow Ridge which makes it so difficult—because of the great distance and the difference in the two worlds, is it not?"

Oh'Dar sighed. "Yes, that is true."

Grateful to finally reach the Far High Hills, they were greeted by Harak'Sar and the guards, who had been waiting for them.

Acaraho noticed immediately that the High Protector was not there to meet them as usual, though First Guard Dreth appeared to be acting in Thorak's place.

"We have quarters already prepared for you," said Harak'Sar. "Though there is still time today, I suggest we wait and convene the High Council tomorrow."

As they were about to head for their quarters, another guard came in with a message that Kahrok had returned—without Khon'Tor.

"What is going on?" Acaraho demanded to know.

"Kahrok, who was exiled from your community, came here a few days ago saying he knew where Akar'Tor was. Khon'Tor left with him."

They waited in silence as Kahrok approached.

"Where is Khon'Tor?" Harak'Sar asked.

"Somewhere safe," answered Kahrok.

"Somehow, I doubt that," Harak'Sar growled.

Acaraho stepped forward. "Kahrok, what have you done? If you take us to Khon'Tor, and he is alive, I will make sure there are no repercussions."

"There will be no repercussions, regardless. Only I know where Khon'Tor is, and if I do not return within a set time, Akar'Tor will kill him."

"What is it you want?" said Acaraho.

Oh'Dar had made his way forward, and Kahrok glanced across, his lip curling. "My old friend; how convenient. The stakes just went up. Send Tehya *and* Oh'Dar with me, and we will release Khon'Tor."

Harak'Sar scoffed. "If you think we would fall for that, you think us fools."

"It does not matter what *you* think. It is up to Oh'Dar and Tehya to decide whether they are willing to take the chance that I am not telling the truth. You have no right to decide for them. Otherwise, I can guarantee you they seal Khon'Tor's death. And it will not be a quick and easy one, I can promise you that."

Acaraho thought quickly. *I need to buy some time to think, and I must get Oh'Dar out of here. And as much as I hate it, Tehya has a right to know what is happening.* Acaraho turned to his son, "Go and tell Tehya what is going on." He lowered his voice to a whisper, "And stay with her there."

With Dreth as his guide, Oh'Dar ran through the passages of the Far High Hills until the guard pointed to a doorway. Oh'Dar ran through it, calling Tehya's name.

She flew from her seat and ran to him. "What are you doing here? Is Khon'Tor back?"

"No time to explain. Where is Arismae?"

"With my parents. Tell me, what's going on?"

"Kahrok has returned without Khon'Tor," he explained.

"Oh, I just knew it was a trap. What does he want?"

"He wants you and me to go with him. If we do, he says he will release Khon'Tor. He is lying, of course."

Tehya bit her lip, thinking for a moment.

"You cannot be considering going?" Oh'Dar asked, seeing the look of determination on her face.

"How can I not go? If there is any chance he is alive, I have to do as Kahrok asks. Otherwise, I cannot live with myself. *What would you do if they had Acise?* Answer that!" she said angrily. "Your father will come up with a plan if he has not already, but he might need time. If Kahrok leaves without us, then Khon'Tor's fate is decided, for sure."

"We are no match for them," Oh'Dar pointed out. "If Khon'Tor is alive, they surely have him incapacitated in some way."

Then they both had the same idea at the same time.

Oh'Dar followed Tehya to the corner, where she asked him to help her. He put his hands out and hoisted her up high. It was just enough for her to reach into the recessed cavity. Her fingers felt what she sought, and Oh'Dar set her back down.

Tehya showed him what she had retrieved, though he had already recognized the hide wrappings.

Oh'Dar unwrapped the hides and nodded.

"We can do this; I know we can," she said. "We have to try, at least."

Oh'Dar quickly emptied the satchel still slung over his shoulder, then grabbed some foodstuffs from the eating area and shoved them in the satchel too. "Remember everything I taught you," he added.

Acaraho was horrified to see Oh'Dar return with Tehya. Kahrok stared at them both as they approached; his eyes narrowed as a twisted smile crossed his lips.

"I imagine you have explained the situation?" Kahrok asked, and Tehya nodded.

"Take me to Khon'Tor," she demanded.

Adia looked over at her mate, trying to control her fear. "Kahrok. Do not do this, please. It is not too late to turn everything around. If Acaraho said there will be no consequences, you can believe him."

"You are wasting your breath, Healer."

"Tehya, I will not allow you to do this," said Acaraho.

She swirled around angrily. "I have already had this conversation with your son. What would you have me do? Turn my back on the only chance there is to save him? Would you do that if you were me? Would you just walk away, *save yourself*? I know you are all thinking they have already killed him, but I do not believe it. He is still alive. *I can feel it.*"

Adia nodded, "He is still alive."

"Akar will not hurt me. He wants me for his own. Perhaps I can bargain with him."

Acaraho shook his head and looked pleadingly at his mate.

"Enough of this. I know you are stalling, trying to come up with a plan," barked Kahrok. "You two, come with me," he signaled to Oh'Dar and Tehya.

Oh'Dar looked at his mother, willing her to read his mind. He mouthed I love you and started to follow Kahrok.

As they neared the exit, Kahrok turned around, "Oh, one last thing, do not try to follow us. I will know, and then they will all die."

"What guarantee do we have you will not harm them anyway?" asked Acaraho.

"None," said Kahrok, looking Acaraho up and down. "But I do not see you have any choice but to take your chances that I am telling the truth."

Kahrok walked over to Oh'Dar, and glaring at him, ripped the satchel off his shoulder and rummaged through it. He found the Waschini blade and threw the rest across the room. "What is this? Some Waschini trickery you thought would give you some advantage? You must think I am stupid," raged Kahrok, angrily tossing the knife across the rock floor where it clattered and finally skidded to a stop near the satchel.

He signaled for Oh'Dar and Tehya to follow him, and they walked out together.

Adia covered her face with her hands. Urilla Wuti came over and put an arm around her.

Acaraho turned to Harak'Sar. "We will give them a slight head start, and then we will track them. Oh'Dar and Tehya will not be able to keep up with Kahrok, so he will have to let them set the pace, which will slow them all down."

"I have no doubt of your abilities, but depending on where he is taking them, you may have a hard time with the tracking. The dry spell has left the ground cracked and with little ability to hold impressions," said Dreth.

Acaraho turned to Urilla Wuti, "I already thought of that. Where is Kweeuu?"

Urilla Wuti's eyes lit up. "He is with Nootau and Iella down at the other end of Amara."

Harak'Sar pointed at Dreth, who dispatched one of his fastest males to go and find the two.

❍

At the far end of Amara, Nootau and Iella were sitting, laughing at the side of a small rivulet. They were dangling their toes in the shallow water for the minnows to nibble.

"It tickles," Iella laughed.

Their joy was interrupted when Nootau spotted one of Dreth's guards sprinting toward them. Kweeuu leaped up, a slow growl in his throat.

"Kweeuu, no!" Nootau shouted, and the wolf stopped in his tracks.

"Come back, Nootau. Your father is here and needs your help."

❍

Nootau saw his mother first and ran to her.

"Where is Kweeuu?" asked his father.

Nootau whistled, and the wolf came bounding in.

"Tehya and Oh'Dar have left with Kahrok." Acaraho explained the situation and his plan to use Kweeuu to track them.

"I understand why they would take Tehya, but I do not understand why they would take Oh'Dar," said Adia.

"Kahrok has disliked Oh'Dar from the time we

were little," explained Nootau. "Many times, I had to defend Oh'Dar against him. He is and always has been a bully."

"Why did you not tell us?" Adia asked.

"I handled it. And I always suspected it would make things worse for Oh'Dar if I told on Kahrok."

"Oh'Dar was likely not part of the plan until Kahrok saw him here," said Acaraho. "Perhaps together, he and Tehya can stall things until we get there."

Nootau frowned, "But Kahrok said not to follow him?"

"We will not. At least not that he will realize. With Kweeuu's help, we are going to track him. Your mother said Khon'Tor is not dead, but we have to assume he is incapacitated. And Oh'Dar and Tehya are no match for Akar'Tor and Kahrok; they may be able to stall the two, but there is no question that eventually they will be harmed. I see no other choice."

Nootau turned to Iella, "I will go with them. I must." Iella nodded and brushed her hand against his cheek, looking deeply into his eyes.

Urilla Wuti said, "There is nothing for us to do here now, except to pray."

Once the search party had left, she and the other two Healers adjourned to a seating area.

Kahrok led them along the banks of the Great River. After a while, he made Tehya and Oh'Dar go on ahead to keep an eye on them and make sure they were not talking. He ordered them to follow the riverbank until he told them to stop.

The heat bore down on them both, and they were grateful for the tiniest breeze that rose from the moving waters. Oh'Dar was watching Tehya for any signs of heat exhaustion, and after a while, he said, "We need to rest."

"You can rest in a while," said Kahrok.

"No, now. I am Waschini, and she is a female. We do not have your stamina. If you truly mean us no harm, then let us rest when we need to."

Kahrok narrowed his eyes to slits but nodded permission. "No talking," he ordered.

"Did you bring anything to eat?" asked Oh'Dar.

"What do you think? Does it look like I am carrying anything? You should have thought of that yourselves."

"We did, but you threw away my satchel."

"You never did know when to shut up. Always talking away. And you never did get rid of that accent. You are not one of us, and you never will be."

"Shut up, Kahrok," Tehya said.

"Oh, the little bird has grown wings? So you talk back now? That is not how I last remember you—when you were throwing up your guts over the mention of Akar'Tor's name. He is looking forward to showing you how happy he is to see you; I will tell you that," and Kahrok licked his lips and blatantly ran his gaze slowly up and down her.

"How much farther?" asked Oh'Dar.

"Not much, come on now, enough resting."

They began the trek again, finally coming to the place where Kahrok said he would take the lead. He stepped in front of them, at this point having every confidence they would follow.

Within a few moments, they were at the little entrance. Kahrok motioned at them to go in. Oh'Dar gave Tehya a long look. "Are you ready?" he mouthed. Tehya nodded, and in they went.

It took longer for Oh'Dar's eyes to adjust. Finally, he could also see the tunnel through which they had yet to pass. As they entered the back chamber, they could see Khon'Tor in the corner, tied up with some kind of lashings. He was slumped over on the ground.

"Khon'Tor." Tehya ran toward him, but before she could get there, a set of muscled arms reached out and roughly pulled her back.

"Let me go," she struggled, twisting her head enough to see it was Akar'Tor who restrained her.

Kahrok stepped out of the corner with a huge tree limb, brandishing it in Oh'Dar's face.

"Waschini, you will get your chance to fight for your life," Kahrok sneered, "but first, we are going to have a little fun." Oh'Dar stood helpless, watching Tehya trying to kick and bite her way out of Akar'-Tor's hold.

Just then, Khon'Tor moaned and moved, his eyes fluttering as he pretended to regain consciousness.

"Adoeete!" Tehya screamed.

Akar'Tor clamped his hand over her mouth. "Yes. He is alive—for now. But he has not eaten for a while, and I am afraid he is a little worse for wear after what I put him through. But do not worry; we will not let him suffer much longer. Only long enough to watch what I am about to do to you. I think he deserves a little entertainment before he dies."

"Akar, let him go. Let him go, and I will stay with you willingly," Tehya pleaded.

"Do you think you can still fool me? You had your chance before. I loved you; I would have cherished you. But no longer. You will be mine and Kahrok's to use as we will—however we want. In a few minutes, when I am done with you and have planted my seed in you, and Kahrok has had his turn, too, then I will kill your Adoeete and put him out of his misery. You will get to watch him die, and there will be no hope of rescue once he is dead."

Akar'Tor reached around, and as Khon'Tor partially opened his eyes, rent Tehya's wrap down the front, almost entirely exposing her.

Oh'Dar was standing beside Kahrok, who, with rapt attention, was watching Akar'Tor manhandle Tehya. Realizing that Kahrok was distracted, Oh'Dar quickly reached into his waistband and pulled out the one thing he had never intended to use and for years had kept safely hidden at Kthama. The shiny pistol Ben had spent hours teaching him to shoot. Each time Oh'Dar left Shadow Ridge, Ben would tuck it into the saddlebags, insisting that it might one day be useful.

Kahrok caught the movement and saw the strange object in Oh'Dar's hand. He managed to strike as Oh'Dar squeezed the trigger, so the bullet only caught him in the thigh. The gunshot was not only deafening, but as unnatural a sound as any of the People had ever heard. Everyone startled and froze, just long enough for Tehya to twist around enough to bring her knee solidly between Akar'Tor's legs.

Akar'Tor crumpled to the ground clutching himself and moaning. As Oh'Dar turned to take another shot, Kahrok managed to reach out a foot to trip him, and the pistol went sliding and scraping out of reach. Oh'Dar tried to catch himself as he fell, but his head connected with the rock floor.

Tehya scrambled over and picked up the pistol. She turned it on Akar'Tor, who, still in pain, was coming to his feet without taking his eyes off her.

"Is that some Waschini weapon? Give it to me," and he slowly stumbled toward her.

"Stop, Akar. I can kill you with this, and I will."

Akar'Tor scoffed, "Hardly. You are weak, like my father. He could not kill me when he had the chance. I have learned that love is a curse, not a blessing. I heard my mother speak of him, and before he met you, he was strong. Powerful. He must have known that this was a trap, but his love for you has weakened him. Made him vulnerable. And now that weakness will cost him his life."

Tehya was holding the pistol firmly in both hands, still trained directly on Akar'Tor as he continued to move ever so slowly toward her.

Oh'Dar was just getting his bearings, and he looked over to see Tehya pointing the gun at Akar'-Tor. Then he looked at Khon'Tor, who motioned for him to come closer. Oh'Dar crawled over and began loosening the bonds.

"Hurry," Khon'Tor urged him, not taking his eyes off Tehya as Akar'Tor slowly closed the distance. At an angle to them, he could also see Kahrok dragging himself toward Tehya without her knowing, leaving a smear of blood behind him.

"You are wrong, Akar," said Tehya. "Love is not what makes us weak. Love makes us strong. Strong enough to stand up to the likes of you. Khon'Tor did not spare you because he was weak; he spared you because you are his son. And no father should have to kill his own son, even to protect the rest of his family.

"But," she continued, the pistol now aimed point-blank at Akar'Tor's chest, "Unfortunately for you, you are not *my* son."

As she started to squeeze the trigger, Kahrok grabbed Tehya's ankle. Tehya instinctively swiveled and fired one shot directly into Kahrok's chest. The recoil knocked her backward, but she regained her footing.

The ear-splitting sound once again echoed in the small chamber.

Khon'Tor, finally freed, lurched forward and knocked Akar'Tor to the ground, wrestling him under control. Akar'Tor was snarling and spitting at him.

"I should have killed you long ago, Akar. But I did not want it to come to this. However, you have made it impossible for me not to end you once and for all."

"I will never stop, not until you are dead and Tehya is mine. And when I am done with her, I will come for *your daughter*," Akar'Tor shouted into his father's face.

"You are wrong," Khon'Tor roared out, "the next time I see you *will be in krell*," and he reached down, took Akar'Tor by the sides of his head, and twisted sharply, snapping his neck.

Khon'Tor let go, and Akar'Tor slumped to the floor. Only when he was certain his son was dead did he turn away.

Oh'Dar had scrambled over to Kahrok's body. A thick pool of red blood oozed from underneath it, spreading across the chamber floor.

Tehya put the pistol down, and holding her torn sheath closed with one hand, ran into Khon'Tor's arms. He caught her up in his embrace.

She gasped out, "I thought they had killed you, I thought I had lost you forever."

"You are safe. We are safe. By the Great Spirit, I vow you will never fear Akar, or anyone, ever again."

"What did they do to you?" Tehya asked, looking at the bruises covering Khon'Tor's body.

"It does not matter. It is over now," he said, holding his mate close.

"Did you know what Akar was up to?" she asked, glancing back at the form crumpled on the ground.

"I knew it was a trap, but I could not pass up what might be the only chance to find Akar. I led them to believe they had bested me. That I was broken, defeated. For some time, I pretended to be unconscious, and I listened as they boasted of their plans to use me to bring you here. I was waiting for the opportunity to free myself before you could arrive. I did not expect Oh'Dar, though," he said, reaching a hand out to the Waschini who was still crouched over Kahrok's body.

Oh'Dar bent down and picked up Ben's pistol.

"It is Waschini," said Khon'Tor, still clasping Tehya to his chest.

"Yes, it is Waschini. My grandmother's mate always insisted I bring it with me, though I never wanted to. Then when Tehya kept having nightmares about Akar'Tor, I started teaching her how to use it. She never fired it until now, though."

Oh'Dar proudly looked at Tehya. "You did well not to let it undo you when it went off the first time," he said. "I tried to prepare you for how loud it would be, and how much kick it would have, and you held on as I had taught you. If it were not for your bravery, we might all be dead by now."

"So this was part of the self-defense tactics you were teaching her?" asked Khon'Tor.

"I apologize," said Oh'Dar. "Please forgive me for not asking your permission. In my gut, I felt it was the right thing to do, but I knew you would disapprove."

Khon'Tor looked down at his precious mate, now safe in his arms.

"Ordinarily, I would have been angry. But that would be foolish considering how this ended. Where did you keep it hidden, though?"

Tehya lowered her eyes in embarrassment. "It was wrapped up, pushed to the back of the high cubby hole, where you put the Waschini blade."

Khon'Tor said, "That explains the startled look on your face when I tucked the blade up there. You were afraid I would find that thing."

"I promise never to deceive you again," she said.

"Neither will I, Adik'Tar," said Oh'Dar.

"Thank you. But I am no longer Adik'Tar," he answered.

Oh'Dar shook his head. "You will always be an Adik'Tar."

Khon'Tor released Tehya and stood over what was left of his son, a son for whose birth he had not been present, only his death.

Tehya tore her top the rest of the way down and tied it in a knot in front. Then she came up behind

Khon'Tor and put her arms as far around his waist as she could reach. She leaned her head against his back and then realized his covering was gone.

"Where is your cloak?" she asked.

"They ripped it off me sometime after Akar hit me over the head. He wore it for a while, mocking me, only he did not realize I knew, as I pretended to be unconscious for some time."

Khon'Tor stood quietly for a moment. His thoughts turn to Hakani. *How long ago you and I were paired,* he thought as if speaking to her. *I tried to make a life with you, but you hated me from the start. Only too late did I realize it was because you found out Adia had been my First Choice. You were never able to let go of your bitterness. Finally, our hatred for each other became all we had. I wonder if our son would have stood a chance had things been different between us. But I will never know. I hope you two are reunited now and that together you will find peace.*

Khon'Tor brought his attention back and broke the silence, "We must return and send guards to retrieve the bodies. No matter their crimes, they still deserve a Good Journey."

The three made their way out of the cave into the bright sunlight.

"Wait," said Oh'Dar. They all paused. The howl of a wolf was just fading off in the distance.

"It is Kweeuu!" and Oh'Dar gave a loud whistle.

Then from around the bend down by the river,

they spotted Kweeuu sprinting ahead of Acaraho, Nootau, and several guards.

The wolf covered the distance well ahead of the others and flew into Oh'Dar's arms, almost knocking him over. Then Kweeuu turned to Tehya and did his best to cover her with huge slobbery wolf kisses. She buried her face in his thick fur and came close to breaking down.

The others came jogging up as quickly as they could. Acaraho embraced Oh'Dar, and holding him tightly, said, "Thank the Great Spirit, all of you have survived."

Then he turned to Khon'Tor. "What happened? You look terrible."

"It was Akar and Kahrok working together. A trap, obviously. Were it not for your son and Tehya, we would all be dead by now. Instead, it is our aggressors who have left this realm. Their bodies are in that cave," he continued, pointing over to the opening, "through a short tunnel and into a back chamber."

"You have quite a story to tell, I am sure," said Acaraho. "Let us retrieve their bodies, and when we are safely back home, you can tell everyone at once."

Khon'Tor nodded. "How do you, Nootau, and the guards come to be here?"

Acaraho almost smiled. "That is, once more, thanks to Kweeuu."

Khon'Tor nodded again and stood with Oh'Dar

and Tehya while the others went to fetch the bodies of Akar'Tor and Kahrok.

Acaraho came out carrying Khon'Tor's wrapping. "Thought you might want this back," and he tossed it across.

Catching it in mid-air, Khon'Tor dusted it off and offered it to Tehya. She shook her head, so he placed the cloak back over his shoulders. As he did, he realized that Acaraho still sported an upper wrap and loincloth.

"It is a new trend. It is catching on with the younger ones," Acaraho said, seeing the glance.

Khon'Tor was not fooled; he knew Acaraho well enough to realize that, while what he said was truthful, the new Leader was showing his solidarity. Khon'Tor had been forced to adopt the style to cover up the wounds from Kurak'Kahn's lashing, and now he did not stand out so badly.

He looked across at Nootau and Acaraho and said, "Thank you."

The guards came out carrying the bodies. "We will have to rig up stretchers," said one. "I do not think we can carry them all the way back without."

Tehya and Oh'Dar sat by the riverbank while the other males constructed two stretchers. Kweeuu ran up and down the shoreline playing in the water and snapping at the fish swimming just below the surface.

"Are you alright?" Oh'Dar asked and put his arm around his friend's waist.

"Thank you for risking your life for us. If you had not brought the pistol—" she stopped.

"It was you who handed it to me to tuck into my waistband. But I will admit that bringing the satchel was a brainstorm. I was right in figuring that Kahrok would not let me keep it and that when he found the Waschini blade, he would not think there might be another weapon concealed elsewhere."

"Will you ever teach me to shoot it with accuracy? I realize I only hit them because I was so close that I could not miss."

"I do not know. We never fired it because the sound would have echoed through the area and immediately be recognized as something never heard before. Which is another reason you should give yourself credit for what you did. There was no way I could prepare you for how loud it would be. You did well to wait for Akar'Tor to get closer and closer, and you would have shot him point-blank in the chest, killing him instantly, had Kahrok not startled you. As it was, Kahrok got the bullet instead."

Tehya looked at Oh'Dar more closely. "I killed someone."

"Yes. But you did not murder him. You know without a doubt that if we had not killed them, they would have killed Khon'Tor and me. And you—you would have had it worse than either of us; they would have made you wish you were dead."

With the stretchers finished and the two bodies

loaded, the group made their way back down the Great River and back to Amara.

It was nearly nightfall. Urilla Wuti was sitting in meditation with the other Healers when her eyes suddenly flew open. "They are coming back. Oh'Dar, Tehya, and Khon'Tor, they are coming back with the others. Somehow they all survived."

The three Healers quickly rose, summoned Harak'Sar, and went to the entrance to wait for the party to return. Adia rushed to Oh'Dar and hugged him harder than she should have, given his slight stature. Urilla Wuti greeted Tehya and Harak'Sar greeted Khon'Tor. "I was not sure we would see you again," he said.

"I was not sure you would, either," Khon'Tor replied. "After Tehya and the others are settled, I could use some cleaning up. And something to eat; it has been several days."

"Go with your mate to your quarters. I will have extra washing supplies sent to you as well as a variety of food. In the morning, we will be anxious to hear everything that happened." Harak'Sar slapped Khon'Tor on the back and sent him and his tiny mate on their way.

Iella rushed into Nootau's embrace. She clasped her arms around his neck and buried her face in his chest. "I was afraid. I was so afraid," she whispered.

He reached up and stroked the back of her hair. "I am right here. Our life is just beginning. I am right here." He repeated it over and over until she quietened.

"Well done, Adik'Tar," Harak'Sar said to Acaraho. "I see you were right about the wolf being able to find them."

"He led us right there. Only, by the time we arrived, Khon'Tor and the others had already handled the situation." Then Acaraho indicated the males behind him who were pulling the stretchers.

Harak'Sar looked back at them. "Akar'Tor and Kahrok?" he asked.

Acaraho nodded.

"I would be lying if I said I was not relieved. And now, you all need to rest. We will catch up tomorrow."

"When will Risik'Tar and Lesharo'Mok be here?" asked Acaraho.

"Shortly after you left, Lesharo'Mok arrived with his Healer and her Helper. Risik'Tar will be arriving tonight, and Paytah'Tar of the High Red Rocks tomorrow evening. Though I do not know if they are bringing their Healers and Helpers. Depending on when the last of them arrive, and if you and they are up to it, we can call the High Council meeting for then. Let me know."

Acaraho told Harak'Sar he was happy with that arrangement, and before returning to their quarters, he and Adia went to retrieve An'Kru from Tehya's mother. Tehya and Khon'Tor were ahead of them and just leaving with Arismae.

Acaraho caught Khon'Tor's eye and nodded, and Khon'Tor nodded back.

Once they had cleaned up and had something to eat, it took Tehya and Khon'Tor only long enough to tend to their little one before they were sound asleep. Tehya lay in her favorite position tucked up against her mate with her head on his chest and her fingers curled in his hair.

Morning came, and the People of the Far High Hills gathered for first meal. Lesharo'Mok and Risik'Tar joined the table occupied by Harak'Sar and the other Leaders who had already arrived. Noticeably absent was the High Protector, Thorak.

Though the others knew that Thorak had been warned to stay away, the recently arrived Leaders did not.

"Where is your High Protector this morning?" asked Risik'Tar. "I did not see him last night when I arrived, either. He is usually on top of such things."

"He is temporarily on a break. He needs a rest," answered Harak'Sar, who was distractedly pushing his meal around in front of him.

Lesharo'Mok and Risik'Tar looked at each other and knew not to press the issue. Over their meal, Harak'Sar explained what he knew of the recent events, including that Khon'Tor's son Akar'Tor was dead. The newcomers listened raptly, then expressed their concern to Khon'Tor and Tehya over what both had presumably just endured.

Later that afternoon, Paytah'Tar of the High Red Rocks arrived earlier than expected. After evening meal, they decided to hold a short High Council meeting. Tehya agreed to watch An'Kru while Adia attended.

Eventually, everyone was assembled in the room prepared by Drust, and they waited for Urilla Wuti to open the meeting.

She took her place at the front, "Welcome, Adik'-Tars of the People. You may wonder why the Overseer, Kurak'Kahn, is not in attendance. There is much to fill you in on because much has happened since we last met some while ago." Urilla Wuti went on to explain that the Overseer had stepped down, and she had been temporarily appointed to serve in his place.

Then Harak'Sar stood and told them the story of Akar'Tor, the Sarnonn rebels, and finally that Khon'Tor had stepped down from leadership of the High Rocks and High Protector Acaraho was now the Leader of Kthama. It took the entire evening to catch everyone up on what had happened in all the communities represented.

After quite some time, Urilla Wuti spoke. "It is late. I am sure that by now you are too tired to take in one more topic. I suggest we adjourn and meet again in the morning," she said.

Everyone left, except Paytah'Tar of the High Red Rocks and Harak'Sar, who stayed a while talking together.

The next morning, the High Council convened again. Urilla Wuti opened the meeting, "You will see that Khon'Tor has joined us. He is here at my invitation to give us some important information. A great deal has happened over the past few days, harrowing experiences, which he, Oh'Dar, and Acaraho will have more to say about. Oh'Dar is here also to present a petition."

"First, however, Nootau'Tor, the son of Adia of the High Rocks, is also present for the first issue we need to discuss, and that is a request from him and my niece, Iella Onida, to be paired."

He and Iella stood to be recognized.

"Nootau is the son of a Healer, and Iella is your niece," said Risik'Tar. "Iella, you took your mother's house name when you became a Healer?"

"Yes. It is our right as Healers to choose which of our blood names we wish to adopt."

"Is there any reason to believe their lines should not be crossed?" he asked next, looking around to the others in the room for the answers.

"I, of course, am aware of Adia's heritage," said

Lesharo'Mok, "just as Harak'Sar and the Overseer will be aware of Iella's. I know of the pairings going several generations back, and from the side of the House of 'Mok, I can see no reason why they could not be paired."

"Nor do I," said Urilla Wuti. "Are there others at your communities who might wish to be paired?" she asked the Leaders at large.

Paytah'Tar spoke up, "We have many who wish to be paired. After I return to the High Red Rocks, I will send a messenger with their names."

"Very well. Now, before I give the floor to Khon'-Tor, I believe Oh'Dar has a matter that needs to be addressed," said Urilla Wuti.

He stood. "I have a request."

Urilla Wuti waved him to the front of the room.

Oh'Dar cleared his throat before beginning, taking a moment to compose his thoughts. "As you know, years ago, I left the People in search of my Waschini family. I found them and have been going back and forth between here and their home for some time now. I know we have heard terrible stories about the Waschini, but I must tell you that I feel they have very little validity. My Waschini family is kind, generous, and thoughtful. They pray to the same Great Spirit as we do."

"They pray to the Great Spirit?" asked Risik'Tar, frowning.

"Not with that name, no, of course not. But their beliefs are the same as ours."

"Go on," said Lesharo'Mok.

"Khon'Tor asked me to start teaching Whitespeak to the offspring and any interested adults at Kthama. My father, Acaraho, supports the idea, so I will continue as Khon'Tor directed. This means I must spend a fair amount of time at the High Rocks. I have also recently been bonded to the daughter of Chief Is'Taqa, and have a life and responsibilities with the Brothers. This leaves me with little time to travel to Shadow Ridge, where my Waschini family lives. They are getting older, and if nothing else, this brush with death at the hands of Akar'Tor and Kahrok has impressed on me even more how precious life is."

They all waited quietly, unsure of where Oh'Dar was going with this.

"My grandfather, the Waschini who a while ago married my grandmother, is well versed in bloodlines and crossbreeding and how to combine lines for both form and disposition. He might be able to help Yuma'qia and Bidzel in determining how best to diversify our bloodlines. My grandmother would be able to help me with schooling the offspring in all forms of the Waschini language."

Risik'Tar looked sharply at Oh'Dar, "Wait. Are you asking if your Waschini family can come and live among us? Or that they live with the Brothers?"

"They cannot live with the Brothers," Oh'Dar answered. "It would raise questions and bring trouble to the village, which is already known to other Waschini. I am asking if they can live at Kthama."

Silence.

"You know what you are asking is against Second Law: No Contact With Outsiders?" asked Lesharo'Mok. "Acaraho, how can you support this?"

"I am well aware that this would break Second Law," Acaraho said, rising to his feet. "But I am also well aware that not everything we have held as sacred is truly that. We have learned that the Rah'hora given to us and the Sarnonn was, in effect, a lie, in that its real purpose was not revealed. It was a maneuver. A strategy designed to keep the People and the Sarnonn apart until such time as we could think for ourselves and act independently. Until we were collectively evolved enough to create the future of our own making. And we could only do that when we began to question everything that we have always accepted as true.

"I am suggesting that perhaps the Second Law prohibiting contact with Outsiders is no different. From comparing our First Laws with Haan's, we know they are virtually identical. The First Laws have always been seen as immutable. The First Laws were created by the Ancients, but the Second Laws were added by later generations."

He turned away, then stepped back to the group. "Not all that long ago, under Kurak'Kahn, this very council amended Second Law to allow Healers and

Helpers to pair and have offspring. As we grow, learn, evolve, so the Second Laws are changing with us."

There was silence until Harak'Sar spoke, "Your grandfather; he is older," said Harak'Sar, a statement not a question. "Are there any younger males who might want to come on such an adventure?"

Everyone stopped talking and stared at Harak'Sar, who continued. "If you remember, we did entertain the idea of bringing in Waschini seed to diversify our blood. And we know it would have to be the combination of Waschini seed and our females. I am not talking about actually mating them to our females. The Ancients figured out how to achieve it, and we can too."

Oh'Dar closed his eyes for a moment. *What is happening? It is one thing to ask someone to turn their whole world upside down and step through a doorway into something they cannot even imagine, but how am I to suggest they might also help us by breeding with us? I would not even know the words to use.*

Lesharo'Mok stood and let out a long breath. "As much as I would like to support you in this, Oh'Dar," he said, "I do not feel that I can. At the very least, it deserves far more consideration than we can give it here. I suggest we table it and revisit it at another time."

Oh'Dar looked at his father and clamped his disappointment down hard to hide it.

"I agree with Lesharo'Mok," said Paytah'Tar of the High Red Rocks. "Khon'Tor, what do you say?"

Risik'Tar stood up. "Excuse me; Khon'Tor is not part of the High Council. He is here to address us, but that is all. Asking his opinion is inappropriate."

"My apologies, but I am still struggling to catch up," said Paytah'Tar of the High Red Rocks.

Urilla Wuti raised her palm to Risik'Tar and said, "Khon'Tor, please. We are anxious to hear the full story of what happened between you and Akar'Tor and Kahrok."

After Khon'Tor had gone through the whole story, he added, "I knew it was a trap, and I was confident that though Akar did intend to kill me, it was not his ultimate goal, which I believed would allow me some time. He had long lusted after Tehya; as you know, he abducted her and held her captive, endangering both her and our offspring, whom she was carrying at the time.

"I blame myself for it coming to this, and the risk to Oh'Dar and my mate. If I had taken care of Akar earlier, it would never have happened.

"Now that I have told you the story, there is something I would like to show you. To do that, I need Oh'Dar's help. Overseer, may the entire High Council please step outside with me?"

Urilla Wuti nodded. The others looked around at each other, then stood and followed Khon'Tor outside.

Khon'Tor took them on a short walk from Amara's entrance to a small valley. He placed a large stone on top of a stump.

"Over to you, Oh'Dar," he said. "Everyone else, please step back with me," and he led them a fair distance away.

Oh'Dar pulled the Waschini pistol from his waistband, took aim, and fired. The rock shattered as the gunshot thundered into the far mountainside and echoed back.

As the shot rang out, the others had instinctively covered their ears and ducked.

"*What the krell*!" shouted Risik'Tar. "What was that?"

Excited voices spoke on top of each other, and Khon'Tor waited for them to calm down.

"That, High Council," said Khon'Tor, "is the Waschini weapon that saved our lives. Oh'Dar had the good sense to take it with him when he and Tehya went with Kahrok. Had he not, no doubt we all would have died. Well, not all," he said quietly, thinking of Tehya. "At least, not quickly," his voice dropped.

Several guards had run into the area, and Harak'Sar raised his hand to stop them. "Please tell everyone there is nothing to be alarmed about. I will explain later. Go."

"May I see that?" asked Harak'Sar, walking over to Oh'Dar, who quickly emptied the bullets from the chamber into his hand before handing over the pistol.

"It cannot hurt you now," he explained.

Harak'Sar turned the shiny metal pistol over and over. He felt the heft of it and sniffed it, his nose wrinkling from the smell of the discharge. Though it was small for his hand, he tried holding it as he had seen Oh'Dar do.

"What is the point of this—*demonstration*—Khon'Tor?" asked Harak'Sar, handing the weapon back to Oh'Dar. "You could have explained it without deafening us, and no doubt, scaring the entire community. It will probably take the rest of the day to calm everyone down."

"I could have. But it would not have had the same effect. The point is, the Waschini are far more powerful than we thought. If they have created weapons like this, who knows what else they can do. We have never had any natural predators, though we have occasionally lost a few to the Sarius snakes. Still, before the Sarnonn rebels, we did not have to fear attack by anyone. This weapon, or one like it, could be used to kill any of us from a distance. It holds devastating power. And who knows what farther-reaching and even more deadly weapons they may in time create." Khon'Tor walked away as was his habit, then turned back, "If they have not already."

He raised his voice slightly. "The rules have changed. Our old beliefs, our old ways can no longer be relied on to serve us. There is no doubt in my mind that we can never let the Waschini know of our existence.

"And I propose we make our alliance with the Sarnonn a priority; we must forge a bond with them that can never be broken. The Sarnonn have cloaking abilities of some type. Perhaps they can use it to hide our existence and theirs from the Waschini forever. And more than that, the Sarnonn will outlive all of us by a measure of generations. It is they who will carry our people forward into the future long after we are gone. We need to interweave our cultures, so the lessons we all learn from our mistakes will survive the forgetfulness of time and not pass from memory—just to rise up and strike us down at another time."

At this point, Adia stepped forward, "The Waschini themselves are not the threat." The others looked at her as if she had lost her mind.

"The Waschini is a name we have given the Outsiders we know. But the Waschini are just one type of their kind. There are others, just as the birds are feathered differently, yet they are all birds. I have been told that some Waschini have darker hair and darker skin, while others have lighter hair and lighter skin. Collectively they are called Hue'Mahns. Waschini is to Hue'Mahns as crow is to bird."

"What Adia is saying is true," said Urilla Wuti. "I have also been given this knowledge."

"So, what; there are different Waschini? What

difference does it make what color they are if they are all the same inside?" asked Risik'Tar.

"That is just the point; they are not all the same. The problem is the mindset that some Hue'Mahns have, not all of them. The mindset that believes in lack, competition, fear, and hoarding creates the damaging currents on Etera. And as their mindset spreads to others, their destructive thinking will multiply to affect all of us. Until recently, how often did we hear of any crimes within our communities? Now it seems they are occurring with alarming frequency."

Adia did not name them, but the others understood that what she said was true. Hakani, Akar'Tor, Berak of Kurak'Kahn's community, Kahrok—even the Sarnonn rebellion, which had taken supernatural intervention to thwart.

"You argue against your son's proposal by pointing out the threat of the Waschini's poisoned thinking, Healer," said Harak'Sar. "Based on what you are saying, it would be foolish to let Oh'Dar bring his Waschini family here."

"I disagree," said Khon'Tor. "That is not what the Healer is telling us. What she is talking about is not a people; it is a mindset, an approach to life."

Risik'Tar muttered, impatiently raising his hands, but Urilla Wuti brusquely interrupted him. "Let Khon'Tor speak," she said.

"We know nothing of the Waschini other than the little bit Oh'Dar has learned and the horror stories that have been passed on to us. This weapon alone should convince you that the worst thing we could do would be to refuse to learn about them. And if I understand what Oh'Dar has just explained, they may have specific knowledge that can help us in solving the problem of our condensed bloodlines."

"One moment, you say we should isolate from them," Risik'Tar said, "never let them learn we exist, and in the next, you are proposing bringing some here and learning about them. Which is it?"

"Learn about them, yes," replied Khon'Tor. "Learn from the Waschini, yes. But on our terms, not theirs. Have no contact with Outsiders, yes; that is Second Law. I have preached more than anyone here about the sanctity of Sacred Law—perhaps too stringently, I now admit. But I propose to you that in this instance, Oh'Dar's people are not Outsiders as we define them. They are his family. And if they are willing to come, to live among us and learn our ways, I say let them come.

"But there must be no misunderstanding. If they come, they can never return to their world. They will never again live in the ways they have known all their lives. It would be a terrific adjustment for them, as it was for Oh'Dar to join the Waschini. And if they are willing to leave behind everything they know and embark on this wild proposal, then I say they are accepting the risk."

Urilla Wuti turned to Oh'Dar. "Do you believe you can make them understand what they would be undertaking? Are you able to get through to them how drastically their lives would change? Beyond their wildest imaginings?"

"I promise you I will not betray our people," Oh'Dar answered. "If I do not believe they will be able to adjust, if I do not believe they will protect us from exposure, then I will not follow through."

"Khon'Tor, is there anything else you want to say?" asked Urilla Wuti, ignoring the sour look on Risik'Tar's face.

Khon'Tor ran his hand through the white streak in his hair and down the back of his head, as had always been his habit.

Adia stopped cold. How many times had she seen him do that very thing? Run his hand through his hair, down over the white streak. The silver streak. Just like Pan's coloring. *By stroking the silver streak in his hair, is he accessing some type of otherworldly knowing?* Adia thought back to how many times Khon'Tor had performed that same gesture, followed by some profound proclamation or decision. Haan's words echoed in her mind. *The Guardians only come through the House of 'Tor.*

Stepping forward again to address the group, Khon'Tor spoke with conviction. "I remember when, not too long ago, this council sat and listened to Kurak'Kahn explain that within seven generations, we would be on the brink of extinction. In that same meeting, we determined that we had two options. One, to interbreed with the Sarnonn. That route is still open to the People, an almost guaranteed option now that we have an alliance with them. The missing piece is to figure out the mechanics, which, in time, we will. The second was to breed with the Waschini. At the time, we believed the Waschini were the catalyst that would usher in the Age of Shadows. We now know this not to be true."

He gestured toward Oh'Dar, "You have just heard Oh'Dar say his grandfather is well-versed in bloodlines, in cross-matching. Are you really hearing any of it? Here we have one of our own, Oh'Dar, practically handing us the opportunity to open a door. A door that may lead to the only other option available to us."

Adia waited a moment for Khon'Tor's words to sink in and take root. Then she spoke once more.

"I agree," said Adia. "And not because Oh'Dar is my son, but because Khon'Tor speaks the truth. And in all the years of his leadership, Khon'Tor has never steered the People wrong."

One by one, Urilla Wuti looked at everyone assembled there. When she got to Risik'Tar, he looked away, unable to meet her gaze.

"We need to vote," she declared. "How many can support Oh'Dar's proposal to ask his Waschini family to join us in our community?"

Slowly, everyone raised a hand until only Risik'Tar was left. Finally, he sighed, and lifting his hand, he joined the others.

Urilla Wuti turned to Oh'Dar, "You have the

blessing of the High Council. However, there is no guarantee your Waschini family will accept, so be prepared for that possibility."

Oh'Dar turned to the High Council members, "Thank you. Thank you for your consideration. I promise you again, I will do nothing to put our people at risk."

After a moment of silence, Urilla Wuti asked, "Is there any other matter to be discussed?"

Harak'Sar indicated that there was, as did Lesharo'Mok, and after dismissing Oh'Dar, Nootau, and Khon'Tor, the Overseer suggested they reconvene inside.

Once back in the meeting room, the others took their seats knowing it might be a while before the meeting ended.

Lesharo'Mok asked to go first. "I have received a request to allow Akule of the High Rocks and his mate, Kayah, to live at the Deep Valley. Unless there is any serious objection, I intend to grant the request."

Acaraho was relieved, though saddened. He remembered Harak'Sar telling him that Akule had asked to move to the Far High Hills to spare Kayah having to endure Khon'Tor's presence and the lingering bad memories at Kthama. But that escape had been blocked when Khon'Tor and Tehya moved to the Far High Hills. He looked over at Adia, who seemed lost in thought. He knew she had hoped that his taking over as Leader would make it palatable for the couple to stay at Kthama.

"I understand the request," said Acaraho. "Do either of them have family there?"

"Apparently, one of Kayah's sisters is paired to one of our males," said Lesharo'Mok. "Most of her family is at the Far High Hills, but she has withdrawn her request to Harak'Sar to live there." He looked across at Harak'Sar, who nodded in confirmation.

As that matter seemed concluded, Harak'Sar spoke next. "What about the matter of our need for a new Overseer? Urilla Wuti is acting in a temporary capacity until we can agree on the replacement for Kurak'Kahn."

"Would you like me to step outside?" Urilla Wuti asked. No one answered, so she stayed where she was.

Paytah'Tar of the High Red Rocks said, "I propose that Urilla Wuti become our permanent Overseer. In this meeting alone, she has demonstrated considerable insight, wisdom, and forbearance. But since I only occasionally participate in the High Council meetings, I would bow to other votes in this regard."

"I support Urilla Wuti as the new Overseer," said Risik'Tar, to the surprise of many.

The others nodded, so Harak'Sar called for a vote, and they unanimously accepted her as official Overseer.

Then Harak'Sar said he had one last matter to bring forward. "As I have told some of you was my intention, I have asked Khon'Tor to be part of my Circle of Counsel. I hope that what we have just witnessed will remind you we cannot afford to lose his guidance and wisdom. Before we left Kthama, Urilla Wuti asked you to come to a decision about whether or not a person's crimes should continue to be held against them after their sentence has been served. If once punishment has been delivered, there is an ongoing price to be exacted. In my mind, other than vindictiveness, there is no reason to deny Khon'Tor a place among us. So the time has come. I am asking you now, will you allow Khon'Tor to join the High Council as an advisor?"

A moment passed, and then everyone stood in agreement to accepting Khon'Tor back onto the High Council. Adia closed her eyes, nearly coming to tears in her compassion for Khon'Tor and by the change in attitude toward him. She suddenly remembered Pan's words about An'Kru. *Already his presence has brought a softening to those whose hearts are open to his influence.*

## CHAPTER 7

After Khon'Tor left the High Council meeting, he went to Tehya's parents. They welcomed him in, and he sat next to Tehya, who was holding An'Kru while Arismae slept.

"Tehya told us about what happened with Akar'Tor and Kahrok," said her mother, Vosha. "I am sorry for the loss of your son," she added, now stammering.

"He was never my son. He may have carried my blood, but in the end, he was nothing more than my enemy. I am grateful that we survived," said Khon'Tor.

"There are no words of comfort for what you have both been through," said Tehya's father, Reckodd.

"Your daughter is a hero. She was braver than you could imagine."

Reckodd's thoughts returned to the moment

when Khon'Tor had selected Tehya as his First Choice. *That male is massive, and our daughter is so small. I have heard he has been a long time without a mate. I pray he will be gentle with her.*

"You are not who I thought you were," Reckodd suddenly blurted out.

Khon'Tor looked up but said nothing.

"I knew you only as a legend, the great Khon'Tor. When you selected our daughter as your First Choice, I was concerned seeing her standing next to you on the platform, so small and delicate, her tiny hand enveloped in yours. She has always been a genuine and gentle soul. I had heard that you were demanding. Fierce even. I feared that your larger-than-life persona would overshadow her needs. But now, as I see you together, I realize you truly love her, and above all else, hold her welfare and happiness as your priority."

"Your daughter has been my greatest blessing. More precious than any accolades I received as Leader of the High Rocks. I am grateful that I did not learn too late what really matters." He looked down at his family, Arismae still sleeping, and Tehya with An'Kru balanced on her knee.

"Our choice is not in allowing change to come to us," said Khon'Tor quietly. "Change comes whether we wish it or not, for change is the nature of life. Our only choice is to embrace it and garner what wisdom we can from the lesson it brings, or reject it and fight against the ever-moving current of life. A current that at its core is designed to carry us to our next greatest good. This, I believe."

⊙

Dismissed from the High Council meeting, Oh'Dar and Nootau stood talking with Iella in the passage-way. "I am so happy for you, brother," said Oh'Dar.

"Thank you. It was brave of you to address the High Council as you did."

"I am a bit shocked that in the end, they agreed to let me try."

"When will you leave?" asked Iella.

"I will stay as long as our parents do. When they leave, I will return with them to Kthama and go to Shadow Ridge from there. I hope I am back for your pairing, though, for your sakes, I hope it is not quite that far off," Oh'Dar added.

Nootau smiled and pulled Iella closer to him. "I want to see An'Kru again."

"You go on ahead and visit with your mother; I am going to get back to my outside work," said Iella. "I will find you later."

The three left in different directions. As he walked away, Oh'Dar's thoughts turned to what he must do next. *It is up to me now. How do I explain to Grandmother and Ben what they would be getting into? I must do my best, or I may lead them to make the biggest mistake of their lives. I pray I am doing the right thing. Urilla Wuti is correct, though; there is no guarantee they will decide to come. In their situation, would I? At their age?*

When Nootau rounded the corner to the Healer's Quarters, his mother was just disappearing through the doorway.

He called out, and Adia, with An'Kru in her arms, turned to wait for him to catch up.

"I have just fetched your brother from Tehya," she explained. Nootau reached out and took little An'Kru from her.

He cradled the offspring in his arms, pulling back the soft woven blanket to see his face. An'Kru smiled up at him, and tears surprisingly stung the back of Nootau's eyes. "He is so precious. There is something special about him."

Then Nootau suddenly asked his mother, "Are you disappointed in me?"

"Why would I be disappointed?" she responded.

"Because I have asked to be paired with Iella. And her life is here, and mine is at Kthama. It makes it complicated."

"It will be quite some time before An'Kru is old enough for you to play with him and guide him. That is more than enough time for you and Iella to figure out your pairing. Perhaps soon you will have little ones of your own. Who knows, your offspring and An'Kru may well grow up together."

Nootau looked taken aback. "I had never considered that possibility."

Adia laughed. "Sorry if that turns your mind about a bit."

"I do hope we have offspring right away, though I know that does not always happen."

"We are not the most prolific of people. Perhaps it goes back to the curse that the story says was put on the Ancients for breeding indiscriminately and overpopulating Kthama."

"You do not really believe that do you?" he asked, wrinkling his nose.

"No," his mother smiled. "I do not believe the Great Spirit punishes anyone. But it seems that, perhaps because of the crossbreeding with the Brothers, it is just natural for us not to bear many offspring. Losing so many of our males during the sickness has also hurt us, and many of our females will struggle to find a mate because they so greatly outnumber the males."

Nootau looked back down at An'Kru again, who suddenly hiccupped. They both smiled.

"Well, on that note, I will let you get back to taking care of my little brother," he said and handed An'Kru back to his mother. Adia cradled the offspring against her shoulder and began patting him gently on the back.

"We will not leave without letting you know. I promise," and Adia kissed him on the cheek.

"I know," he said and watched her turn to enter

the Healer's Quarters. He smiled as he faintly heard little An'Kru hiccup again.

Several days later, Acaraho and Adia decided it was time to return to the High Rocks.

Adia had spent as much time as she could with Urilla Wuti, but they had not discussed their separate meetings with Pan, as they did not want to exclude Iella from the circle. The more they were together, the more Adia found herself growing fonder and fonder of the young Healer and was deeply pleased with Nootau's choice of mate.

*Oh'Dar and Acise. Next, Nimida and Tar, and Nootau and Iella. My heart's desire is coming true—for my offspring to find true happiness and someone to travel through life with. Who knows what the future will bring for us. And for An'Kru. But as long as I know my offspring are happy and safe, I can weather any storm.*

Khon'Tor met with Acaraho and asked how the atmosphere was at Kthama. Acaraho said there was some struggle as they were adjusting to the change in leadership, but that it was to be expected.

"Do you have a message about Akar'Tor that you wish me to deliver to Haan?" asked Acaraho.

Khon'Tor had already thought about this. "With

your permission, I would like to travel to Kthama and meet again with Haan and his people. But since that will be sometime in the future, please tell him what happened. And tell him I am sorry it came to this."

"He will understand. It will hurt him to know that Akar'Tor is gone, but Haan knew that his son was living a tortured life. And he is no doubt with his mother now; perhaps that will give Haan some solace."

Khon'Tor nodded.

"Harak'Sar told the High Council that he is forming his own Circle of Counsel and has asked you to serve as one of his advisors. Have you accepted?"

"I have not told him so, but I am leaning toward it."

"I hope that you do," Acaraho said. "Do not let your regret over the past keep you from accepting it. It would be a shame to lose the ongoing benefit of your wisdom and experience, and the High Council does not meet as often."

Khon'Tor studied Acaraho's face.

"We have walked a long road together, you and I," he said. "I like to believe it has been mutually beneficial. Or at least it was until I—"

"I will never forget standing with you against the Sarnonn attack," Acaraho interrupted. "I believe that was our finest moment, though I believed it would be our last."

Khon'Tor nodded. "Safe journey, Adik'Tar Acaraho, Leader of the High Rocks."

Then he turned and slowly walked away.

The time came, and Adia, Acaraho, and Oh'Dar finally stood making their goodbyes in the entrance at the Far High Hills. Nootau did not want to leave Iella just yet and was staying a bit longer.

Kweeuu wound himself around Oh'Dar's legs, nearly knocking him over. "Kweeuu, stay. Stay with Tehya," he ordered, and the giant wolf left to sit at Tehya's feet.

"If all goes well, I will be back in a couple of months with the rest of my family," said Oh'Dar as he bade farewell to his brother.

Khon'Tor offered Oh'Dar his hand and then wrapped him up in a bear hug. When Oh'Dar was released, he was laughing, and the others laughed with him as he staggered a bit before regaining his balance.

"Thank you, Oh'Dar," said Khon'Tor. "For everything."

Harak'Sar's guards escorted the travelers to the tunnel that ran underground along the Mother Stream. The coolness of the passage was a welcome escape from the last summer heat, and the cool rock felt good under their feet as they padded along. They traveled at a leisurely pace, stopping on and off to rest, tend to little An'Kru, and enjoy each other's company.

○

Once Acaraho, Adia, An'Kru, and Oh'Dar had disappeared from view, the others turned to go about their business. Harak'Sar stopped Khon'Tor before he could get too far away.

Khon'Tor turned back.

"You did not respond to my request for you to join my Circle of Counsel," Harak'Sar said.

"I apologize. I have been thinking about it and would be honored to accept."

"Good. I will call a meeting in a day or so. There is much to discuss and much about life here for you to catch up on."

Out of the corner of his eye, Khon'Tor noticed two young males talking to Tehya, who was waiting for him. His blood started to rise as he saw one of them embrace her.

"Excuse me, Adik'Tar," he said to Harak'Sar and strode over to them.

One of the males noticed him coming, and they all turned to face Khon'Tor.

"Adoeete!" squealed Tehya in happy excitement.

Khon'Tor eyed the two young bucks.

"I want you to meet Alderis and Selval." Khon'Tor looked them up and down, and the two exchanged glances.

"These are my brothers," she explained.

Khon'Tor relaxed, and his expression softened. *Of course. I should have noticed the smaller build.*

"They are both watchers, placed in the farthest of our regions. They do not get home much, but that is how they prefer it. That is why it has taken so long to introduce you."

Khon'Tor nodded to both of the young males. "My apologies," he said. "I—misunderstood the exchange."

"We understand," said Selval. "We know our sister is exceptional. If I had a mate such as she, I imagine I would also be possessive."

Alderis chimed in, "We are just coming in from a long stretch of duty. After we clean up, we will be visiting our parents. We are also anxious to meet little Arismae, whom our sister has just told us about. Perhaps we will see you at evening meal."

Khon'Tor nodded, "I will leave you to your reunion."

He walked away with no destination in mind. He passed Nootau talking with First Guard Dreth and gave them both a nod. *My son. Nootau is my son. It is just as well he does not know. There is no benefit to it; it would hurt him and perhaps cause problems between him and Adia—and Acaraho, who is a far better father to him than I would have been. Perhaps in time, these regrets will pass. I pray for the dawning of that day.*

Dreth was addressing Nootau. "The wooded hills are the best place to spend time alone with your

Saraste'. There is a small trail that leads up the north side, and if you follow it far enough, you will come to a large oak. The smaller path to the left will lead you to a beautiful shady grove of fruit trees where the late summer flowers are in bloom. I was just there a few days ago, and it is very pleasant now."

Nootau nodded. "Thank you. I will surprise her with a visit there."

Khon'Tor smiled as Dreth slapped Nootau on the back, and he continued on his way.

In the Healer's Quarters, Urilla Wuti sat in a training session with Iella. They had just finished a Connection, and Iella was trying to regain her bearings.

"That was not as hard to shake off as some of the other sessions," she said, rubbing her eyes.

"I took you deeper than ever before, yet you seem less affected than the last time," Urilla Wuti said.

"It seems that over the past few months, I have gotten stronger, but, oddly, also more sensitive. I feel others' emotions more easily. Perhaps that has something to do with it?"

Urilla Wuti thought for a moment. "When the next High Council convenes, I am going to call a separate meeting of the Healers. I need to know if the others are feeling an increase in their sensitivities."

"You think all Healers are experiencing this?"

"I suspect they may be. When Kthama Minor was opened, there was a tremendous shift both in Adia's abilities and mine. It is not out of the question that it might have affected the rest of us." *I am still not sure whether Pan's appearance to Nootau means he has dormant Healer abilities. But if so, they should surface soon enough,* Urilla Wuti thought to herself.

Iella nodded. "You have not mentioned being confirmed as Overseer."

Urilla Wuti sighed. "It is a high honor, but it comes on the heels of another's pain. I am humbled by the faith they have placed in me, but it is difficult to embrace without reservation."

Iella did not pry any further, but she surmised it must be something to do with Kurak'Kahn.

"When do you think the next meeting will be? And yes, I am asking because I am anxious for my pairing with Nootau to happen." She smiled over at her aunt.

"When I hear from the other communities which of their males and females wish to be paired, I can give you a better answer."

Nootau was traveling the path Dreth had described to him, searching for the beautiful setting where he hoped to take Iella. He walked absentmindedly, mulling over the events of the past few days, grateful that his brother and everyone else had survived. He stopped suddenly and turned his head to listen. He looked up the hillside, but, seeing no one, he continued.

Nootau soon found himself at his destination. It was just as the First Guard had described it, quiet, secluded, peaceful. Wildflowers rimmed the grove, and a sweet breeze carried their scent over the verdant ground. Large trees offered enough shade to cool the late summer heat. *This is perfect; I cannot wait to bring her. How beautiful it would be for us to be paired here. If no others are seeking Ashwea Awhidi, perhaps Urilla Wuti would consider blessing our union here.*

As he was about to leave, he heard a heavy thud as something fell from the treetops overhead.

Nootau froze. Ahead of him, barely beyond striking distance, was a gigantic Sarius snake. Its almond-shaped eyes were cold and almost calculating. A long, sinuous tongue whipped in and out of its mouth, no doubt tasting Nootau's presence.

*Do not move.*

Nootau heard the words in his head. He stood perfectly still, barely allowing himself to breathe. He locked eyes with the creature, realizing there was no way to escape should it decide to attack him.

Nootau had heard stories of Sarius snakes but had never seen one. They were reclusive and adaptive, changing the pattern and color of their scales to match their surroundings. They would gather on branches, waiting for something to walk underneath.

Usually, they dropped right on top of their prey and quickly coiled their bodies around the victim, squeezing out their life in a matter of moments before swallowing them whole. How this one had not landed on top of Nootau was a miracle in itself.

*What now?* Nootau was thinking quickly. *I cannot stay motionless forever.*

"I could try and save you," said a voice from farther up the hillside. Nootau almost startled but caught himself in time. Hating to take his eyes off the predator still coiled in front of him, he slowly slid them to the side enough to confirm what he already knew.

Thorak.

Far enough away to be safe himself, Thorak was standing watching Nootau's predicament.

"If I save you, will you leave the Far High Hills and Iella to me?" he taunted Nootau.

Nootau returned his eyes to the snake, trying to figure some way out of his dire situation. It started to rise, preparing to strike.

*When I tell you.*

There was the voice in his head again. Nootau's heart and mind were racing. Not knowing what to believe, he said a prayer and committed to listening to the voice and whatever it said next.

*Get down. Now.*

Against all reason, knowing the motion could well trigger the snake's attack, Nootau ducked.

A spear whizzed overhead and caught the Sarius

snake directly in its terrible open mouth. The giant creature writhed and coiled and struggled, trying to dislodge the weapon. Nootau sprang back as dust and debris flew everywhere while its giant body flailed and whipped about. It finally ended up too close to the edge of the trail and rolled down the hill-side, too far out of range to be any farther threat.

Nootau turned to see who had thrown the spear. Dreth stood several feet behind him.

"I do not know what you are doing here, and with a weapon, but am I happy you are!" Nootau's knees were shaking.

Dreth walked over to the edge to make sure the snake was long gone, if not dead. Then he walked back and looked up the hillside where Thorak had been standing, taunting Nootau.

"I was actually on my way out to hunt when I saw you going down the path I had told you about and decided to make sure you found the right place. You were lucky I was here. Had I not been you would now be worked into the belly of that monster. I am sorry, Nootau, I had not thought to warn you of them. They are seen so seldom. And I never would have suggested this spot if I had any idea there was one nearby."

"I know that," said Nootau.

Dreth closed his eyes, letting out a heavy sigh as he shook his head. "I must report this to Harak'Sar. It saddens me deeply; I would never in my lifetime have believed that Thorak could behave so. There is no excuse. There can be no more excuses. Come," and the First Guard motioned for Nootau to return with him to Amara.

❦

Thorak had retreated up the hillside when he saw Dreth sneaking up with the spear. He was not sure if Dreth had seen him, and if he had, he hoped the First Guard had not heard him tormenting Nootau. *What have I become? It is my job to protect others, not bargain with them to save their lives.* Thorak was consumed with shame, and it was a long time before he felt able to return home.

❦

When Thorak did return to Amara, he went straight to Harak'Sar. "I must speak with you, Adik'Tar," he said, his voice low.

Harak'Sar stared at him, waiting for him to continue.

"I wish to surrender my commission as High Protector. I no longer have any right to the honor of bearing such responsibility. I am requesting that I be relegated to a lesser station, one more becoming to the level of trust I deserve."

As Dreth was bound to do, he had reported the entire incident, and Harak'Sar already knew what had happened.

The Leader had his speech planned. He had been prepared to denigrate Thorak, shame him, and admonish him for his cowardly and unforgivable actions, but now that it was time to do it, he could not.

The truth was, Harak'Sar had been personally cut to the core by Thorak's behavior. The High Protector had served Harak'Sar faithfully for several years. It was inconceivable to have his honorable service end in shame such as this, yet there was no doubt that Thorak had done as Dreth had reported, and now this confession only added to that.

Harak'Sar opened his mouth to speak, but all he could say was, "I accept your resignation. Report to the First Guard tomorrow, and he will assign you new duties."

Thorak kept his head bowed, refusing to look at Harak'Sar, refusing to see the disappointment he knew was in the Leader's eyes. He backed away, turned, and left for his quarters, where he stayed the rest of the day, berating himself for his foolish actions.

Having seen the exchange from a distance, Dreth approached Harak'Sar.

"He was like a son to me," said the Leader. "I cannot begin to tell you the number of times he made me so proud. He was the first to step up to help others. He always took the hardest duties, sparing his males before himself. How could it come to this, to his behaving so? I would not have said it possible, yet here we are."

Word of Thorak's dishonorable behavior would travel through the ranks like a javelin, piercing the hearts of all those who had looked up to him. It was a terrible loss, especially as it followed a difficult period.

"When will it end?" asked Harak'Sar, not expecting an answer. "Will things ever return to normal?"

He sighed and walked away, asking himself what would cause someone to act so. *I have never loved a female enough to drive me to such ends. Khon'Tor is the same; he feels the same about his Tehya. What is it like to love someone that much? I will never know, and perhaps it is for the best. I love Habil; she is a great comfort to me, and I enjoy her company. But I am grateful I do not care so much that I could lose myself like that.*

It did not take long for word of Thorak's actions and Nootau's brush with death to spread throughout Amara. Before long, everyone was talking about both. Iella heard about it from her aunt and immediately went to find Nootau.

"Why did you not tell me about this?" she asked, grabbing his hands in hers.

"I did not want to denigrate Thorak, so I did not know how to tell you."

"I want to be paired immediately. I do not want to wait any longer," Iella said.

"Shhh. You are upset, and I understand. I would

feel the same way if something like that happened to you," he said.

"No, I am serious. Now. Let us go and find Urilla Wuti now and have her pronounce Ashwea Awhidi over us. Tonight!"

She led him back down the passageway to the Healer's Quarters, where she had left Urilla Wuti.

"Overseer," Iella said as they entered.

Urilla Wuti gave her a quizzical look. "Overseer? Since when do you address me as Overseer?"

"When that is the capacity in which I need your help. Please, please pair Nootau and me. Now."

Urilla Wuti looked upon her niece with soft eyes. "Knowing what has just taken place, I understand your emotion. Please, sit down."

Iella reluctantly followed Urilla Wuti to the sitting area, Nootau in tow.

"We need to confirm with the record-keepers that this pairing is permitted," Urilla Wuti said once they were seated.

"But you said there was no reason for it not to be," Iella cried out.

"Yes. And I still believe that. But just because I am Overseer does not mean I can throw all protocol to the wayside. And you may wish to consider whether you and your mother want to travel to Kthama for you to be paired there. That way, Nootau's family can also share in your joining."

Iella had calmed down enough to see the wisdom in what her aunt was suggesting.

"Alright. I am sorry; you are correct," she said.

Nootau put his arm around her.

"Very well," conceded Urilla Wuti. "I will ask Harak'Sar to send a messenger with your request. When he returns, we will speak with your mother and make plans. But it may take a while for the researchers to answer."

While Urilla Wuti was waiting for word from the researchers, Harak'Sar told her that several of the other communities had sent the names of the males and females who wished to be paired. Unfortunately, there were not enough males to go around.

Urilla Wuti sighed, "I am glad we will have new pairings. But some of the maidens are going to be disappointed."

## CHAPTER 8

Snana and Noshoba were playing with their sister's wolf cub, Waki, next to one of the Great River's shallow tributaries. Suddenly the cub pricked up her ears, letting the hide toy fall to the ground. Just then, Snana and Noshoba also heard it. A horse whinnying from some distance. They looked over to see Pajackok watching them from the tree line, mounted on his horse, Atori.

"Look, look," Snana whispered. "We should go and tell Papa." She whisked up the wolf cub and the toy, and they started back to the village.

"Wait," Pajackok called out.

The urgency in his voice startled Snana. Not knowing what to do, she stopped and warily looked back, worried that the young brave might start out toward them.

Pajackok dismounted and headed down the incline. "I mean you no harm, Snana," he called out.

"Please wait for me. I just want to talk. I do not blame you for being afraid. I have behaved very badly, I admit."

Snana looked him up and down; he looked a bit drawn, and his clothing was scuffed up. "Where have you been living? We have all been worried about you." She pushed Noshoba behind her as she spoke.

"Worried? Probably not worried, but I am sure you have all been talking about me."

Pajackok kept coming closer. Snana took a fleeting glance around, looking for something to use as a weapon. The brave saw what she was doing and paused.

"I just want to talk," he said, his palms out.

"Papa will be here in a minute. You can talk to him."

"You are very pretty; do you know that?" Pajackok said.

"Please, you are scaring me," she said, attempting to stop the trembling in her lower lip and her hands. Wanting to buy time, she tried to keep the conversation going.

"Where have you been staying? We were told you headed west."

"I have been on my own. I built a shelter not too far from a little stream. It is very nice if I say so myself, but I am lonely; I need company. Where is Acise? I miss her."

Snana stopped herself from saying that Acise did not miss Pajackok, realizing it would anger him.

"She is not in the village. She has taken some hides and clothes to Kthama as a present for the Healer's new offspring."

"Would you like to come and see my shelter?" he asked.

A chill ran up Snana's spine. She turned and pushed the cub into Noshoba's arms, whispering, "Find Papa and tell him Pajackok has returned. Bring him back here as quickly as you can."

Noshoba nodded and took off with Waki pressed tightly against his chest.

Pajackok said nothing as he watched the boy leave.

"No. No, I would not like to see it," Snana answered. "I have to go, Pajackok. My parents are waiting for me. Please leave me now."

She looked over her shoulder to see how far Noshoba had gotten. While her attention was turned, Pajackok closed the short distance between them and grabbed Snana around the waist, lifting her up off the ground.

Snana immediately started kicking and screaming, trying to claw and bite Pajackok anywhere she could. Noshoba heard her and stopped. Then he heard her yell out, "Run, Noshoba, run!" and he took off once again, as fast as he could, the cub dangling in his arms.

Pajackok tightened one arm around her waist and covered her mouth with his other.

"Stop it. Stop it!" he yelled into her ear. "If you do

not stop struggling, I will have to hurt you. And that is the last thing I want to do!" She tore at his hands but could not free herself.

"I mean it, Snana," he warned her. "You are coming with me one way or the other."

Snana slowly tried to calm herself. *If I can just stall a little longer, perhaps they will get here,* she thought.

"Now stop struggling. I am going to remove my hand, and if you scream again, I will leave. But I will be back, and the next time I will come for Noshoba. Is that what you want for your little brother? To be taken from his family and his village? Never to see your father or mother again? It is not Noshoba I want, but the choice is yours; which is it to be? You, or your little brother? You did not see me coming until I was nearly upon you, and you will not see me next time, either; I promise. It is getting late; make up your mind."

Pajackok slowly removed his hand from her mouth. Snana did not scream or struggle.

"Come with me then," and Pajackok took her by the hand and led her back to his horse. "And stop scuffing your feet to leave a trail; you are not fooling me."

By the time help arrived, Snana was nowhere to be found.

Is'Taqa and his braves scoured the area. The dry season had made tracking difficult, and though they searched for hours, they could find no sign of either Pajackok or Snana.

Chief Is'Taqa paced around the shelter, Honovi and Noshoba watching him. "Why would he take her? Does Pajackok think it will force Acise to leave Oh'Dar for him? Is he going to use her to bargain with? All his actions are just making things worse for him."

Noshoba was desolate. "I should not have left her."

"You did the right thing," his mother comforted him. "Your father will find her; do not worry," she said, desperately wanting to believe what she was saying.

Soon Tac'agawa, Pajackok's father, asked to enter. His face was drawn. "I came as soon as I heard. Tell me this is not true."

"I am afraid it is. Do you have any idea where your son might have taken her?" the Chief asked.

"No. Until now, he has never strayed far from home."

"Noshoba heard Pajackok say that he has built a shelter by a small stream. We believe to the west, which is the direction the People's watcher saw him head when he first left."

"It could be anywhere. I wish I could help you better," Tac'agawa replied. "This is not like him. I am not trying to make excuses, but neither his mother nor I can understand his behavior. I will be glad to join your trackers when next they go out."

"It is nearly nightfall, so no more progress will be made today. It is as if Snana and Pajackok just disappeared," Is'Taqa said. "Unfortunately, he is one of our most skilled braves. If he wants to disappear, there is no one more able to do so than him."

Big as he now was, Honovi pulled Noshoba onto her lap, trying to distract him by waggling a piece of hide to make Waki chase after it.

"Snana is smart," she said. "She will figure out a way to escape. I do not, for a moment, believe he would harm her. Is it possible that as he said, he is just lonely?"

"It is possible," said Is'Taqa.

Pajackok's mother suddenly also stepped into the shelter.

"Perhaps we should go outside," Is'Taqa suggested, and they went to stand by the evening fire.

"I am so sorry," said Tac'agawa. "He will not harm her; I am sure of that."

"Regardless, he has taken her against her will, and it is difficult to say what might happen when a man is prepared to do that. We can only pray to the Great Spirit that he is simply lonely for a friend."

That evening, clouds rolled in, bringing a massive thunderstorm. Is'Taqa lay quietly in the dark next to his mate, listening to the thunder and the heavy rain pelting against their shelter. Noshoba was asleep next to Honovi, and the wolf cub was cuddled up in the crook of her knees.

Despite his turmoil, Is'Taqa tried not to toss and turn. *As if the dry spell did not make tracking them hard enough, whatever clues we might have found later with which to track Pajackok are now washed away. I have no idea how we will find her. Had they been on the other side of the Village, the People's watchers would have seen it all. I can only pray that she uses her wits and finds a way to escape, and pray she can somehow signal her where-abouts or make her way back home.*

Snana rode in front of Pajackok. He had lashed her to him by the waist and tied her hands in front, just loose enough to clasp the horse's mane for support.

She could feel his body heat against her back and tried to sit forward, but there was not enough space. The hard strength of his body was pressed up against her, and his thighs were hugging hers. She tried to keep her thoughts from moving ahead. *Is he really just lonely? Or is this a ploy somehow to kidnap my sister? Or is he thinking of keeping me captive forever?*

The moonlight cast enough light for them to continue traveling, and they rode on through the rest of the night. He stopped only for a few short breaks to give them both some relief but kept her tied to him at all times, though at a distance. He said little, occasionally gruffly reminding her that it was her choice to come with him, and should she change her mind, he would gladly carry out his threat to take Noshoba instead.

Snana tried to memorize where they were going, but sudden cloud cover and intermittent rain made it impossible to make out any useful landmarks.

The first rays of sunlight broke over the horizon, burnishing the turning leaves. The little warmth they brought was a comfort to Snana as she was soaking wet from the overnight rain. She could not control her shivering, though she tried her best.

"You are cold," he said. "We will be there by nightfall. I will make a warm fire, and you will be able to dry off." They were the first kind words he had said to her, and in spite of herself, she found them comforting.

They continued on, and unable to fight her exhaustion, Snana dozed against the warmth that Pajackok's body provided her.

By twilight, she was chilled to the core and feared she might become sick. Just when she felt she could not stand it any longer, he pulled Atori up and said, "We are here."

Pajackok unlashed Snana and slid to the ground. He reached up and lifted her down.

"There is no sense in even thinking of running away," he warned her. "You are cold and tired and hungry. Inside, there is warmth and food and shelter. Be reasonable and accept your fate."

He led her into the shelter, which was, frankly,

very well built, and she was glad of its protection. He led her to a corner and sat her down, then gathered some of the dry kindling and firewood stacked inside. Before long, he had a strong fire going, and she inched closer to its welcome warmth. Pajackok reached up, pulled down a blanket that was hung against one of the side beams, and wrapped it around her. Before tucking her feet underneath, he rubbed them to stimulate the circulation.

Snana eyed him cautiously, trying to figure out what he truly wanted from her. His kindness was confusing, but she was too tired to stay awake any longer. Finally, she let herself lie down and fall asleep.

She woke to the smell of food. Pajackok had made a hearty meal from stores gathered while he was living there.

More alert, Snana took in her surroundings. The shelter was more spacious than she had imagined it would be. It was expertly designed, with a hole in the peak for smoke to escape and ample space for storage and to move around. *Did he build it this large because he was planning on bringing Acise here? It looks permanent—as if he intends to live in it forever.*

"Here," he said. "Have some more food, and then you can rest again."

Snana eyed him suspiciously as he served her another portion.

"Why are you doing this?" she finally asked.

"I told you," he said, as he went to the corner and

neatly restacked the unused firewood. "I am lonely. I need companionship. Female companionship," he added.

"Exactly what do you mean, female companionship?" she dared ask, fearing the answer.

Pajackok stopped what he was doing and turned back to her, his dark eyes piercing hers. "You know what I mean."

Snana closed her eyes.

"I am only here because you forced me to come."

"I do not see it that way. I gave you a choice. You chose."

"It was not much of a choice," she retorted.

"Nonetheless, it was a choice," he countered.

"They will not find you here," Pajackok added, sitting down across the fire from her. The day was cool, and he picked up a stick and stirred the flames into greater life. The stones at the fire's perimeter were starting to collect the heat and radiate it out into the room.

"I made sure the route I took would leave no trail. Make peace with it, Snana," he said, locking his gaze on hers. "I am not as bad a man as I have recently appeared."

Snana studied him while he was speaking. Highlighted in the flickering firelight, his features were attractive, handsome even. *He was one of our most skilled braves. He could lure any female he wanted into choosing him; why is he forcing me to be here?*

"In the morning, I will show you the best places

to hunt and gather. I will help you make baskets for cold weather storage. I have several hides in progress and more than enough firewood stored and dry. We will pray for a mild winter, but, regardless, we will be safe and warm."

"You can never return to the village now, after what you have done," Snana said.

"I never intend to. I have made my choice, just as you have. Now it is up to both of us to make the best of it."

"I am not Acise."

"I do not want Acise."

"That is not true," Snana blurted out, immediately regretting it.

"Believe what you want. I said I missed her, and I do. But you cannot keep loving someone who does not want you."

"So instead, you kidnap someone else who also does not want you?" She once again wanted to snatch back the words the minute they were out of her mouth.

"You are feisty; I like that. You will come around, you will see. I can wait. Now I am going to the spring to catch some fish. Do not try to leave. You are far from the village and any other people. You have no supplies and no idea which way to go. Here there is shelter, warmth, food, and protection. This is your life now, and the sooner you accept it, the easier it will go for you."

He stood up and fed more wood to the fire.

"Think of what we will need to winter over. Look around, see what hides I already have, and let me know what else you think we might need. It is too wet to do much outside, so best you stay here today and keep warm. When the forest dries out, you can explore—I am sure you will want to gather some plants and roots for medicines. I will help you prepare and dry whatever you need to."

The fire refueled, Pajackok lifted down a gourd of water hanging above them and set it down beside her. Then he picked up his fishing spear, mounted his horse, and rode off without looking back.

Once he was gone, Snana finished the rest of her meal and lay back down, wrapping the blanket around her for further warmth.

*Is he right? Are we so far away that they will never find me? Or is he lying to keep me from trying to escape? One thing is true; I do not have any idea where I am.*

Before long, now full and dry, she slipped into a deep sleep.

Snana's eyes fluttered open when Pajackok returned, a good-sized turkey dangling in his grasp. He held it up higher and said, "No fish, but just as good. I will be outside preparing it."

Snana sat up and realized she needed to relieve herself. She stepped outside and looked around, the blanket still wrapped around her shoulders.

It was a beautiful area. The late summer wild-flowers had faded, their colors replaced by the turning of the leaves. She had to admit that Pajackok had chosen the location well; steep, high slopes provided shelter from the west, from where the weather came. Firewood was stacked far enough away and out of the clearing to keep it as dry as possible. There was another firepit a little way from the shelter, much like back home. It was familiar in so many ways, and in spite of herself, she found it inviting.

Snana walked around looking for some privacy, aware that Pajackok was watching her from where he was working. He caught her eye and motioned to an area to the south. She nodded and quickly found a little path through the woods to a secluded area. A small rabbit jumped out from a pile of fallen leaves and shot across her path, startling her. When she had finished, she followed the path a bit farther and found a late crop of raspberries growing in a sunny area created by an opening in the dappled canopy. She stuffed as many as she could into her mouth and then looked around for something to collect the rest in. She was surprised to see a small woven basket hanging on a tree branch close by. Standing on tiptoe, she could just reach it, so she filled it up and returned to the shelter.

Pajackok looked up from dressing the turkey to watch Snana as she returned. He smiled, seeing that she had found the basket and filled it. She offered him some raspberries, but he shook his head and held up his hands, which needed a good washing. "Thank you, though; I will have some later."

She turned and went back into the shelter, brushing the leaves from her clothes before she entered.

They spent the day mostly in silence. Snana slept some more and tried to imagine what her family was thinking about her disappearance.

Back at the village, Acise and her traveling companion were returning from Kthama. They had brought Honovi gifts of honey and goldenseal from Adia. As Acise approached, she sensed that something was wrong. A group surrounded her father and mother, and she hailed them as she picked up speed.

"Thank goodness you are safe," her mother said, opening her arms in welcome. Her father took the carrying basket.

"What has happened? What is wrong?"

"Pajackok has taken Snana," Is'Taqa said.

Acise's eyes flew wide open, "What? When? How? Where is she?"

"We do not know where she is. But we do not believe he will harm her. He said he needed companionship."

"*Companionship!* What kind of companionship?" Acise blurted out. Overcome, she sank to her knees.

Honovi stooped down and put an arm around her shoulder, speaking softly.

"Please try to calm your fears. I know it is hard. Wherever Snana is, everyone here believes she is safe. Your sister is smart; she will survive, and if there is any way she can escape or let us know where she is, she will. In the meantime, the braves are out looking for her."

Acise stood, her face in her hands. Noshoba came up and patted her back. She opened her eyes and pulled him into her, hugging him tightly.

"Please, tell me what happened."

Her mother told the story while Acise listened quietly.

"If only I had been here, perhaps he would have taken me instead."

"There is no point in thinking that way. We can only do our best to find her. And pray to the Great Spirit for her protection."

"How did he get her to go with him? Snana is strong; she would have fought him."

Honovi sighed.

"There were signs of some struggle," Is'Taqa explained, "and from the tracks, we could see she was trying to leave marks in the ground. At least she was moving under her own power when she left with him."

Ithua brought something over for Acise to drink. "This will help calm you down."

"Ithua, I am late." Despite the situation, Ithua

smiled. "If you are pregnant, it will not hurt the baby."

Honovi looked up at Is'Taqa, and then at her daughter. "This is happy news."

"Oh'Dar does not yet know. I was going to wait until I was sure," Acise said.

"Of course. Hopefully, he will return soon," said Ithua.

Over the next few days, the Brothers were fully occupied with Snana's abduction, and a pall hung over the village.

Everyone went through the motions of living, and every day the braves went out searching, but spirits were low, and there was little joy to be shared.

Within a few days, Oh'Dar returned to find everyone so solemn. Acise ran into his arms as he arrived.

"What is wrong?" he asked, pulling her back and searching her face.

"Snana. Pajackok has kidnapped Snana."

"What! When?" he exclaimed.

Acise told Oh'Dar the rest of the story, including how far and wide they had looked for her.

"I have received permission from the High Council to offer my Waschini grandparents the opportunity to come and live at Kthama, but I cannot leave you now. Let us see what happens. There is some time yet before the cold weather sets in."

Time passed. Though hope of escape kept her going, Snana had created a routine for herself. In the morning, she would rise, wash, and prepare something to eat. Then she would work on weaving baskets or honing rocks for spearheads and arrows. She had made a respectable set of bow and arrows for Pajackok, realizing that whether she liked it or not, they were in a kind of partnership, and if they were to survive the winter, she had to do her part.

One morning, Pajackok returned with a wood carving and handed it to her. "It is not as fine as the one the Waschini brought you, but I hope you like it."

Snana put her hand out and took the primitive wooden comb. She turned it over and over, realizing he had worked hard on refining it as much as he could. She looked up at him and quietly said, "Thank you."

"Here, let me help you."

She stiffened as he sat down behind her and gently pulled her hair back. Then he leaned forward and put his hand out, and she returned the comb to him. He carefully drew it through her hair, patiently separating out the tangles. That done, he continued to pull the comb down in long slow strokes. Although she hated herself for it, she closed her eyes and enjoyed the pleasure of having her hair brushed. Against her will, a small sigh escaped her lips.

*No, no, no*, she thought to herself. *You must not surrender to this. If you do, you will never escape. This is not the life you want for yourself, no matter how kind he seems to be and how beautiful it is here. Momma, Papa, Noshoba, Acise; they must all be worried sick about me. Oh, how I wish I could let them know where I am, but how can I when I do not know myself?*

As he once more brought the comb gently down, he leaned in just enough that Snana could feel his warm breath on her neck. His hard thighs, pressed against her hips, felt like a protective cradle. She could smell his male scent and feel the heat radiating off him. She felt her insides clench, and a wave of longing spread through her middle.

"That is enough, thank you," and she reached back to take the comb from him.

"You are beautiful, Snana," Pajackok said softly. "How could I not have seen it before." He reached back around her and handed her the comb, letting his fingers linger on hers for just a moment. Then he rose and returned to his work.

Snana tossed her head as if to shake off the pleasure she had felt at Pajackok's ministrations. The rest of the day, she buried herself in her chores, trying to push the morning's experience from her mind.

Evening fell, and they sat together at the outside fire, the flames licking the air and taking the chill out of the fall evening. Stars blazed overhead in a clear sky, though the lack of cloud cover made for cooler nights. Far overhead, an owl hooted.

"I found a honey tree," Pajackok said, breaking the silence. "I will gather some soon if you like."

"I do not like honey."

"Everyone likes honey."

"Well, I do not. So save yourself a lot of bee stings and do not waste your time on my account," Snana added. She looked over and saw him smiling and shaking his head. For some reason, his smugness irritated her no end.

It was a long time since Snana had brought up his kidnapping of her. "How long are you going to keep me here?" she asked.

"Until you no longer want to leave," he answered, looking at her across the dancing flames.

She closed her eyes, blocking out his handsome face. "Then I will be here forever," she answered, eyes still closed.

"Either way, you are mine now," he said and poked at the fire some more.

She glared at him through the dark. "I will never be yours," she snapped. Then she rose quickly and went inside the shelter.

Later that evening, Snana lay as quietly as she could, covered up on her sleeping blanket and feigning sleep. After some time had passed, Pajackok came in, and she held her breath as he stood over her.

He squatted down beside her as she counted her heartbeats. He smoothed her hair back from around her neck, and the touch of his hand sparked feelings she did not want as her traitorous body cried out to return his caress. Then he pulled her blanket up higher and tucked it in around her. He softly patted her hip and went to his place across the shelter and lay down.

Snana lay as still as she could until his breathing told her he was asleep, and then slowly rolled over until she could see him. She gave in to her desire to study him unawares.

His long black hair was splayed over his broad shoulders. Even though the weather was turning a little cooler, he wore only a light tunic. Snana's eyes hungrily followed the lines of his form, from his chiseled jawline, over his biceps and the muscles in his chest to his rippled core. Then they wandered farther to— *Stop it*, she admonished herself and reluctantly turned over. She slept fitfully for the rest of the night.

Knowing the winter weather was nearly upon them, Snana had worked hard to gather what she needed for her supplies. She was proud of the medicine stores she had collected. Again, she had to compliment Pajackok, at least to herself, on the area he had selected. Truly everything they needed seemed to be within easy reach or just a short walk away. The creek bed was abundant with stones, and she enjoyed walking up and down the banks, searching the shallow water for exactly what she needed. She had claimed a little space in the corner of the shelter for her personal items—the comb he had made her, a few bright blue feathers, and the particularly pretty stones that had caught her eye.

One morning she returned from an early walk to find part of a dripping honeycomb set on a large flat stone next to her other things. Looking around to make sure Pajackok was not there to see, Snana ran her fingers through the gooey sweetness and licked them clean, closing her eyes with the joy of the rare treat. Though she tried to ignore the honeycomb, over the next few days she kept going back to it until, finally devoid of anything edible, it disappeared as silently as it had shown up. It was never spoken of.

One early afternoon, after she had finished her morning chores, Snana was inside straightening up the fire stones when she heard a loud crack outside followed by a heavy thud.

She ran out of the shelter to find out what had fallen and saw Pajackok trapped under a huge tree branch. He was moaning and struggling to free himself from the crushing weight that rested on his legs.

"I will help you." She hurried to his side and tried to lift it off of him. She panted as she tried yet again, to no avail. "What can I do? Please, tell me what to do," she pleaded.

Pajackok garnered enough control to look around and pointed to a sturdy branch not far away. It looked to be a weight she could manage.

*Of course*, Snana thought, then quickly gathered it and placed it under the log that trapped him.

Finding a suitable stone, she pushed and pushed until it was in place, and using her full weight on the other end, leaned down and was able to raise the log far enough for Pajackok to drag himself out. She released the lever once he was clear, and the limb came thudding back down.

Pajackok rolled over, clearly in pain.

"Let me see," Snana said.

He motioned her away, but she ignored him.

"No, let me see!" she yelled. With difficulty, he lifted his hips so she could pull down the leg wrappings, repositioning his breechcloth to cover his manhood. His thighs were already reddening, and there were multiple scrapes and some deep cuts. She pressed gently along his thighs, knees, and legs, then carefully eased his wrappings back in place and said, "Can you make it to the shelter? I do not feel any sign of broken bones."

Pajackok lifted himself up on one elbow and attempted to stand. He could not even make it to his knees, so he half crawled, half dragged himself back to the shelter. Once inside, Snana dusted him off as best she could, then took her own blanket and added it to his own.

"Remove your leg wrappings and breechcloth, then please take this and cover yourself, so I can tend to your wounds," she said, handing him the small piece of soft hide she was planning on turning into a pouch for her comb. She turned to her medicines, giving him time to do as she had ordered. When she turned back, she stifled a gasp at how much worse the wounds were than she had first surmised.

She gently cleaned them and dabbed on some healing salve. She could see Pajackok was trying to hide his pain and knew she was adding to it by her actions. When she was finished, she gave him some willow bark to chew on.

"Rest as best you can," she said. "Hopefully, this will give you some relief from the pain."

Pajackok nodded but said nothing. She knew it was all he could do to keep from crying out in front of her. His wounds were severe, but she was thankful nothing was broken.

"The cuts are deep, and there will be considerable bruising. But nothing is broken, and for that, we must be grateful."

That evening, Snana pulled her sleeping blanket closer to him so she could tell if he woke up in the night and needed more willow bark. She awoke to find she had moved closer to him during her sleep and was pressed up against his back for warmth. She started and quickly moved away, hoping he had not noticed. The hides were now ready for use, and she vowed to bring them in by nightfall.

Over the next few days, Snana faithfully tended to Pajackok. He tried to refuse her help, saying he was fine, but she knew otherwise. She checked him frequently for infection and cleaned and dressed the wounds as often as he would let her. Finally, he declared that enough time had passed and healed or not, he had to get back to his work.

As he had attempted several times before, he tried to rise, pulling up first one knee, then the other, until he was ready to stand. Finally, this time he made it to his feet but almost lost his balance.

Snana was instantly at his side, placing her hands on his chest to steady him. He leaned on her shoulder for support. She caught the scent of his hair as it feathered over her face.

"I think I am alright now," he said. His hard muscles rippled under her hands as his eyes met hers. His mouth was just inches away, and a flood of desire welled up through her. For a moment, silence hung heavily between them, and she realized she longed for him to press his lips against hers. And more.

But he did not.

Instead, he straightened himself up, thanked her, and hobbled out of the shelter under his own power.

"Where are you going?" she called out after him.

"To the stream. I desperately need to clean up, as I am sure you have noticed."

"I will come with you; I do not want you to slip and fall."

"As you wish," he said, "But I cannot afford to get my hides wet, so you are forewarned if you see anything you do not wish to see."

Snana blushed. "I am training to be a medicine woman," and she raised her chin and followed him. "So it is nothing I have not seen before," she lied.

She watched from the bank as Pajackok carefully picked his way through the shallows into the deeper water. He had stripped off every one of his coverings and left them next to the stream. "I am not looking," she called out, turning her head and relying on sound to let her know if he got into trouble.

"I thought you said it was not anything you had not seen before," he chided her.

"I assure you; it is most certainly not."

"Is that so? So, we are all the same to you? One man is as good as the next?" he teased as he carefully splashed the cool waters over himself. "Do you have any soapwort?" he asked.

"Yes, I will be right back." Snana rose and ran to get the soapwort. She kept her gaze high as she tossed it to Pajackok, refusing to give him the satisfaction of anything lower. Turning her back while he lathered up, she took her seat on the riverbank and waited. After a few moments, there was some dunking and more splashing as he rinsed off.

"Alright," he said, "the water is cold, and that will have to be good enough. You can look now."

Snana turned in his direction and gasped. He was naked from head to toe.

Realizing she was staring, her cheeks filled with color, and she scowled as she looked away, "You said I could look!"

"You said it was not anything you had not seen before," he countered.

"Oh!" she huffed and rose up. "Just for that, you are on your own now," and Snana stormed back to the shelter, kicking a flurry of leaves ahead of her. She could hear Pajackok chuckling as she went.

That evening, wrapped in way more hides than was necessary, Snana moved her sleeping blanket as far away from his as she could get it.

"Are you still mad at me?" he asked, breaking the stillness of the dark once they were settled down for the night.

"Shut up. I am sleeping."

"No, you are not."

"Well, I am trying to. That is, I might be able to if *someone* would keep quiet," Snana replied.

"So you are mad," he said.

"For me to be mad, I would have to care what you think or what you do. And I do not. Now lie there and *be quiet*."

"You are very bossy. Has anyone ever told you that?" Pajackok asked.

"Constantly," she answered. "Now go to sleep."

A moment later, he said, "It is cold. Come over here and sleep next to me like you did the other night."

Snana let out a heavy sigh. *Oh no. He knows I did that.* "I do not think so. Sorry. Get yourself another hide," she said.

"There are not any more. You have them all over there with you."

She sat up and grabbed one of the hides and tried to toss it across the shelter at him, careful to avoid the fire pit, but it flopped on the ground between them. She lay back down and turned her back to him.

"Thanks," he said. "But I have a better idea."

She froze, hearing him get up and drag his blanket over to hers. He lay down next to her, only inches away. *Dear Mother*, she thought.

"There. Now we can both sleep better," Pajackok said, stretched out behind her.

She waited for him to press himself up against her, but he did not. *Whatever game he is playing is not going to work*, her mind told herself. But her body was not convinced.

The next night, and the next, Snana moved her sleeping blanket away, and once she was settled in, Pajackok moved his next to hers.

During the daytime, he dutifully took care of his responsibilities, and on and off showed her little kindnesses—a bouquet of wildflowers, a lovely rock or feather to add to her collection. Knowing how much she loved seeing their colors, when they were working outside together, he would point out the birds. Once, he brought a wooly caterpillar and sneaked it onto her arm, knowing it would tickle her as it crawled up to her shoulder. She laughed until she said she could not take it anymore, and he carefully picked it up and set it back in the brush. From time to time, she would allow him to comb her hair, refusing to admit how much she enjoyed his closeness and the accidental touch of his hand on her neck. She found herself craving his touch.

Then one night, he closed the distance and scooted right up against her.

Snana froze, and her breath hitched. Slowly, he snaked his arm around her waist and pulled her back tightly against him. "Shhh. Relax. Go to sleep," he said. Desire flooded her, and her breathing deepened. She could feel every bit of him pressed up against her, his strong arm caging her. In spite of herself, Snana found she felt safe. Protected. Even cared for. But sleep? Sleep would be an impossibility.

"Pajackok," she cried out softly.

"Hmmm?" he said sleepily and pulled her in closer, burying his face in the back of her hair. Her insides clenched as her body betrayed her, begging her to surrender to what she could no longer deny was her desire for him.

"Do you still love Acise?" she dared to ask.

He whispered into her ear, his warm breath brushing her neck, "No."

He withdrew his arm from around her waist and brought his hand up and softly caressed the side of her cheek, nuzzling her ear. Then whispered, "Now I love another."

She turned enough to face him and looked into his eyes. Tears welled in her own as she realized those were the words she was hoping to hear. Sensing her willingness, he slowly leaned in and lightly swept his lips over hers, barely making contact. Then he pulled back and searched her face. When she did not turn away, he kissed her again, ever so lightly. Another moment and then another, still soft and gentle, but a little more intense.

Then, reason no longer in control, she wrapped an arm around his neck and pulled him in harder and returned his kiss with an urgency that surprised her. Their passions sparked, he rolled her over toward him and rested his thigh on hers.

"Oh," she moaned against her will, burning to feel more of him against her.

He stopped and looked into her eyes. He smoothed her hair from her forehead, then drew his hand down softly over her cheek, ran his thumb lightly across her lips, then continued on down her graceful neck, and on until he found and cupped one of her mounds, gently teasing the tip. She placed her hand on the back of his head and drew him even harder into her. He loosened her tunic and let it slip to the side, exposing her curves. He looked down, "You are so beautiful." He continued to gently worry one tip, feeling it respond under his touch.

"If you want me to stop, I will," Pajackok said. When she did not answer, he reached down and pushed down his leggings. He kicked them off and then sat up enough to pull his tunic over his head and toss it out of the way.

He then lay back down beside her. He kissed her ear and moved down her neck, then farther, farther, and heard her catch her breath.

Slowly he moved his hand up under her skirt to cup her between her legs, where he discovered she was ready for him. But he wanted her more than ready. He wanted her to need him inside her as desperately as he needed to be. He touched her gently, feeling her raise herself against the pressure of his fingers, wanting more. He found her entrance and gently began to explore her welcoming wetness. He quickly realized she was a maiden. He closed his eyes, glad she could not clearly see his face in the dark.

"Are you sure you want this?" he said as he continued his caress. "I must hear you say it. I should have realized, but I did not know you were a maiden," he chastised himself.

She answered him by pulling off her skirt and shrugging off her tunic. Finally, skin to skin, there was nothing to stop them from what they both wanted.

Pajackok slipped over on top of her, keeping his weight supported as she willingly parted her thighs, inviting him to give her what she now admitted to herself she desperately wanted. She wrapped her legs around him and pulled his hips down against her until he was pressed hard against her entrance. A motion away from taking Snana, he leaned in and kissed her. Then he whispered her name and pressed himself once, hard, into her. He felt her give way and a small squeak left her lips.

Holding back how deeply he wished to ravage her, he instead stopped and held his place inside her.

Snana opened her eyes and looked at him. Despite her heavy breathing, she managed to pant out, "Are you not supposed to move or something?"

He chuckled, "Yes. But I must be sure you want me to continue."

"Oh yes, please," she said, and then he started to move slowly and easily, entering and withdrawing. Entering and withdrawing. She moaned and turned her head to the side, her hands digging into his biceps. They moved together, lost in their joining, finding the rhythm to express their feelings for each other. Feeling her tension building, hearing her breath catching, he patiently waited for her release, and then, at last, the sounds of ecstasy overcame her in wave after wave. As he felt her finally relax, he began moving in earnest until he found his own release.

Finally spent, Pajackok carefully withdrew himself. He reached down and found the blanket Snana usually covered up with and pulled it over her before he flopped down next to her. They lay there in the dark for some time, neither saying a word.

Finally, Snana rolled onto her side, her back to him. She reached behind and pulled his arm around her, into the position that had sparked their love-making. She laced her fingers in between his and let out a long slow breath. Before long, her breathing changed, and she was asleep.

The next morning, Pajackok awoke to find Snana gone. He threw off the covers, and running out of the shelter, skidded to a halt, startling her.

"What?" she said, surprised, looking up from the firepit, a blanket around her shoulders. "I thought I would make breakfast out here so as not to wake you."

Pajackok turned away to hide his reaction. Only then did Snana realize he had thought for a moment that she had left. Finally run away.

She wanted to say something to reassure him. "Come, sit here with me. Together, let us plan our day," and she patted a spot next to her by the fire.

Without Snana saying another word, they both realized she had no intention of trying to escape. However he had done it, he had worn her down. Through weeks and weeks of kindness and attentiveness, he had won her heart in spite of her vows against it.

Later that evening, after a long day, they turned in again and curled up together. Before they drifted off, she said quietly, "I just want you to know, I am happy here; I no longer wish to leave." Then she continued, "My only regret is that I cannot let my family know I am alright." Then she raised his hand to her lips and kissed it. She snuggled back in against him and sleep quickly came to them both.

The next morning found Pajackok bringing his horse into the camp and tossing a blanket up over its back. He had assembled some pack baskets and was wearing his warmest buckskins.

"What are you doing?" Snana asked, somewhat alarmed.

"I am taking you home," he said, continuing his work without turning to face her.

"I do not want to *go home*. I am home; I thought you knew that." She walked over and stood in his line of sight.

"You said you wanted your family to know you were alright. The only way to do that is to take you back."

"But I do not want to go back."

Pajackok finally stopped what he was doing and gave his attention to her. He took her hands in his and stared into her dark eyes. "It is the only way for them—and me—to know the truth."

"I have told you the truth."

"Regardless, I am taking you back. You were right. I gave you a choice, but it was not a fair one. I brought you here against your will. Now I am taking you home. You will then be free to choose. You can stay in the village and resume your life there, and if I am able, I will leave, never to bother you again. Or you can choose to return and make a life with me here."

He released her hands and went back to his preparations.

Finally satisfied that all was done, he said, "That is the way it has to be. Please get ready to leave. Dress warmly and bring extra layers so when we bed down, you will be comfortable. We can make the journey more enjoyable this time, but that means it will take us longer to get there."

## CHAPTER 9

As time passed, the Brothers had to admit defeat and gave up their search for Snana. Oh'Dar had delayed his departure for Shadow Ridge, but, eventually, the pressure of the dropping temperatures was making him nervous.

One morning, as he was making preparations to leave, a commotion caught his attention. Nearly everyone in the village was heading in the same direction and shouting. Acise, Honovi, and the others were soon running after them.

A rider had approached, but not alone; a woman was clearly perched in front of him. It was Snana and Pajackok.

Acise cried out in relief. "He is bringing her back. Pajackok has brought Snana back!" Then she broke down, turned, and cried in her mother's arms.

Pajackok slowly rode into the village, dismounted, and lifted Snana down. She hurled herself at her mother and Acise as the rest of her family surrounded her.

Pajackok's father approached and stared word-lessly at his son. His mother threw her arms around him and hugged him tightly.

"I made a mistake," Pajackok said, looking at his father across his mother's embrace.

"You made a big mistake, son," but Tac'agawa stopped at that.

Is'Taqa was hugging his daughter as she assured everyone that she was alright.

"There is nothing I can say to right my wrongs," said Pajackok. "For what it is worth, I am sorry. I realize how badly I behaved, and I understand the severity of my actions."

Chief Is'Taqa studied the young brave's face. *He was one of our best. Skilled, respected. What do I do now? I need your wisdom, Chief Ogima. Please tell me how to handle this.*

Honovi and Acise took Snana's hands to lead her away.

"No!" she cried out, digging in her heels. She broke away from them and ran back to Pajackok, putting her arm around his waist and leaning her head against his chest. "Please do not harm him. He brought me back. I am safe. He was nothing but kind to me."

She knew what they were thinking. "Pajackok did nothing to harm me. He brought me back of his own free will. You must believe me," she begged.

Is'Taqa frowned hard and looked at his partner.

Honovi shrugged; she also had no idea what was going on.

"Right," said Chief Is'Taqa. "Everyone, relax. Let us all calm down while we sort this out."

"Pajackok, go home with your parents. Snana, come home with us. Emotions are too high right now, and we all need some time."

"I do not want to go home with you. I want to stay with him," Snana argued, looking up into Pajackok's eyes as he returned her gaze.

"Oh, my goodness, child, just for once, do as your father says." Honovi took her daughter's arm and tugged her away from Pajackok's side.

"Go with them," Pajackok said. Snana looked up at him with alarm.

"I will not leave, I promise." He repeated himself, "I *promise*."

She leaned up and kissed him, at which point her mother turned and raised her hands in the air. "Can someone please tell me *what* is going on?" she pleaded to no one in particular.

Is'Taqa eyed Pajackok with suppressed anger. "Snana, do not take long. We are expecting you at our shelter very soon."

Acise walked up to her sister, 'Please come, Snana," she begged, refusing to look Pajackok in the face.

"I will be along shortly. I will," Snana said, touching her sister's arm and then pulling her in for a hug. "It is alright, I promise. I will tell you every-thing later," she whispered.

Finally, the crowd dispersed, and everyone went on their way. Snana soon joined her family.

Later, when they were sitting alone at the evening fire, Oh'Dar said to his partner, "I do not know how it has happened, but I would say those two are in love. As in, really, truly, *in love*."

Acise shook her head. "I know; I thought the same thing. But let us see, now that Snana is back home with us. Perhaps it was only an infatuation, a twist that evolved because of the circumstances. As for Pajackok, he always was a fine brave. A good man, really. Now that Snana has returned and we know she is safe; I hope everyone can find forgiveness for what he did."

"Time will tell."

Acise rested her head on Oh'Dar's shoulder. "You must continue preparing for Shadow Ridge. I believe everything will be fine here."

"Yes, it is time for me to leave," agreed Oh'Dar, looking around them, "but I am glad I saw Snana return; I did not want to leave you while she was gone, and now some sort of balance has been created. That, and the cold weather is coming."

The next morning he finished preparing what he

needed for the journey, packed his saddlebags, and set out for Shadow Ridge.

Acise, Honovi, Noshoba, Snana, and Chief Is'Taqa watched as he rode out of sight.

Back at Kthama, Bidzel and Yuma'qia had completed their work and decided on the best matches for those wishing to be paired. They sent word to Urilla Wuti, who sent word to the communities, and a date was set for the Ashwea Awhidi. It was agreed to hold it at Kthama, as, once again, only the High Rocks had room enough for a celebration this large.

Along with the others hoping to be paired and their families, Iella, Nootau, Drista, and Urilla Wuti prepared to travel back to Kthama. Nootau was looking forward to seeing his parents and his brothers again. Especially little An'Kru.

When everyone arrived at Kthama, Acaraho personally showed Urilla Wuti to her usual quarters. She stepped inside with the same feeling of coming home as she had experienced before.

"Adia will be over to visit you shortly; I am sure you have much catching up to do," Acaraho said as he left to check on Drista.

He entered to see her standing talking to her daughter.

Drista looked Acaraho up and down. "I can see

again where Nootau gets his build and his good looks."

Iella once again rolled her eyes skyward.

Acaraho smiled. "There will be a guard posted down the hall for your convenience, only to ensure you have everything you need. Once you find your way around, I will be happy to have him reassigned."

"Thank you," she said. "It is beautiful here."

"Preparations are being finalized, and as soon as the others arrive, we will start the celebration."

High Protector Awan had been working diligently with Mapiya to prepare for another fair number of guests. Temporary rooms had been assigned, stores stocked, work schedules organized.

It all reminded Mapiya of the pairing of Khon'Tor and Tehya so long ago. Bittersweet memories flooded through as she unseeingly cut up the vegetables in front of her. She thought back to the years when one day was much like the rest. When life was predictable. When they still had their beliefs for comfort. When they believed they were formed by the Great Spirit out of the dust of Kthama's walls, or so it had gone. Her attention was brought back to the present only when Nootau approached to introduce Iella to her.

"Iella, this is Mapiya. Do not believe what anyone else says; she really runs everything around here."

Mapiya chuckled and shook her head. "What can I do for you both?" she asked.

"I am looking for my mother and An'Kru."

"You will find them outside. She and Pakuna are down by the riverbank. You know, your mother's favorite spot where all the lilies bloom in the spring."

Nootau nodded and took Iella by the hand.

As the couple neared the river, Nootau spotted his mother with An'Kru and Pakuna. Suddenly bunnies and squirrels shot out everywhere. A flock of birds flew from the trees nearby, though a lone crow remained, looking down over the females and the little offspring.

An'Kru laughed and reached out at the receding forest creatures.

"What was that about?" Nootau asked, watching a shoal of fish scattering away from the shore. Pakuna raised her eyebrows and looked at Adia, waiting for her to explain.

"I do not know. It happens now whenever I take him outside. Creatures come out from everywhere—rabbits, squirrels, ground chippers, birds, you name it. My only explanation is they are attracted to An'Kru. When anyone interrupts, they leave. Except for that crow. He is stubborn."

"Is it the same crow that comes each time?" Nootau asked.

"You know I can't be sure," his mother answered. "Perhaps?"

"Maybe you should ask Haan about this. Maybe

it is part of the prophecy. You know, the whole Seventh of the Sixth thing." Nootau walked over, reaching down for An'Kru, and Adia released him to his big brother.

As Nootau cuddled the offspring, An'Kru reached up and waved his little arms, to which Nootau chuckled. Then he looked into An'Kru's silvery grey eyes and frowned.

"You have a funny look on your face; what is it?" Iella asked.

"A strange feeling just came over me. Like I know An'Kru. That I already know him. Who he is, but in a different way. Almost as if we had met before, only as —" Nootau shook his head.

Adia and Iella exchanged glances.

"Are you alright?" Adia asked.

"I do not know. I felt as if time shifted. That for a moment, I was somewhere else, and something had already happened that has not happened yet. Am I losing my mind?" Nootau squeezed his eyes shut, and Adia could see he was deeply upset by whatever had just taken place.

"Let us go to Urilla Wuti," Adia said. "I am anxious to see her again, anyway."

Nootau handed An'Kru back to his mother, and they went in search of the Healer, only to find she was resting; their questions would have to wait. Seeing he was still upset, Iella said she would look for Drista and give Nootau time to gather his thoughts.

Alone in his room, Nootau walked around, questioning everything that had just happened. Eventually, he lay down and stretched out. He looked around the familiar surroundings and thought that soon he and Iella would be lying here together. The thought made him feel better, and he closed his eyes.

He awoke with a start and looked around at the splendor that surrounded him. The colors, the fragrances, even the feel of the ground under his feet were more alive than anything he had experienced before, except for the one time Pan had visited him. *I am back in wherever this is.* He looked around for Pan. Off in the distance, against a backdrop of the bluest sky he had ever seen, he could see the familiar mountains that surrounded Kthama. A magnolia tree, delightfully fragranced, appeared to his right, and suddenly, a large crow landed on one of the top branches. Black feathers shimmered in the sunlight; a dark eye peered down at him.

Nootau waited, and it seemed as if there was all the time in the world—as if he could stand there forever, happily. For eternity. So he waited next to the magnolia tree, whose sweet fragrance was delightful in and of itself.

A figure started to form, and Nootau smiled in anticipation of being in her presence again. But instead of the colossal shape of Pan materializing in front of him, this was smaller, without her bulky figure.

Within moments, a tall male stood there. Nootau stared, wide-eyed, at the most magnificent creature he had ever seen or could ever have imagined. His hair was silver-white, long and flowing as if an invisible wind played with it, and his eyes were the color of winter storm clouds, but almost as if lit from within. His coat had the same shimmering light as Pan's and was thicker than usual. However, his build was that of the People.

Nootau froze. "I know you."

"And I know you, brother."

"How can this be. It is you, An'Kru— But you are —were—so little— I just left you."

"Yes. In your time, I am a tiny offspring. But I will not always be."

Nootau felt more loved and accepted than he had ever been before, not even by his mother. This was something that surpassed understanding.

"Where am I? Where is Pan?"

"Pan is not with us for this visit. But she is still watching over you. It was her voice you heard on the path with the Sarius snake."

"She saved my life."

"You are protected, Nootau. You have many years yet to live on Etera before you join me here. And you will meet with Pan again, I assure you. But that is not what I brought you here to say."

Nootau was confused. He knew he loved Iella

and wanted to return to be with her, yet he did not want to leave An'Kru's presence, not ever.

As if reading his mind, An'Kru said, "You can go back to Etera now, Nootau. You and I will have an eternity to spend together when it is time. But that time is not yet. When you are ready, ask your mother to explain this visit to you. As for your path, trust that you are guided. Do not be concerned about where you and Iella should live. Do not be concerned about what your relationship with me is supposed to be.

"As you can see, I turned out fine. Let go of your fears of failing the Great Spirit; your heart is pure— one of the purest ever—and it will guide you. Return to Etera. You come from greatness, and you have greatness within you. Enjoy your life with your beloved Iella, listen to your heart, your wisdom, and have faith that everything is unfolding as it should. You will unequivocally know when the time has come to be at my side."

Nootau had no sooner nodded than he was back in his body in his quarters at Kthama. He shook his head and looked around. Everything looked dim as if seen through a fog. He breathed deeply, trying to recreate the vitality he had just experienced. He rubbed his hands over the sleeping mat, trying to feel the softness of the blades of grass under his feet again. Instead, everything was a pale reflection of the reality he had just left.

Nootau lay there and kept replaying over and

over what he had just experienced. Then he said out loud, "I promise, An'Kru. I will live my life and trust that all is unfolding as it should."

Later at the evening meal, Nootau asked about his Waschini brother. "Is Oh'Dar coming for the Ashwea Awhidi?"

Adia shook her head slowly. "No, I am sorry. We received word that he has left for Shadow Ridge. I know he will be disappointed not to be here for your pairing, but considering the distance, I do not think he will return in time."

Nootau thought a moment. "It is alright. He is doing what is his to do next."

"You are your mother's son, that is for sure," Nadiwani smiled at him.

"I come from greatness," Nootau said.

Adia chuckled, "Well, on that note, I think we should discuss living spaces. I assume you and Iella will use your quarters while you are here?"

"Yes," he said.

"Good," said Mapiya. "That tells us what we need to do next."

"Are you going to fill it with dried flowers and all manner of pretty female things?" he asked.

"Yes, we are," said Mapiya, chin up, and they all laughed.

"Good," he smiled. "Iella will love it."

Once again, the Great Chamber was brimming with the People. The somber mood created by Khon'Tor's leaving had started to lift as friends and relatives were reunited from across the communities. Acaraho had arranged for more time for socializing, as well as for some of Chief Is'Taqa's braves to come and put on a drumming and dancing display. Some of the females shared their finest weaving designs with each other, and Nimida had set up a place to display her latest tool-making and continue Tehya's legacy with ideas for new wraps.

Having been encouraged to bring their own creations, travelers had brought whatever light-weight items they could for trading.

Adia looked out over the group and said to her mate, "I am not sure what this has turned into, but they all seem to be enjoying it immensely."

Acaraho nodded and smiled at those passing by. "Yes, I agree," he answered.

After the first night had passed and the Ashwea Tare was completed, the time came to hold the pairing ceremony. The researchers had worked hard to come up with the best matches for everyone involved. The eligible males and females sat nervously, looking around the room, wondering with whom they would be paired. Many of the females looked worried, realizing there were not enough males to go around.

Nimida and Tar, and Nootau and Iella were sitting together looking comparatively relaxed. Those couples who had asked to be paired were under far less stress than the others. Nootau and Iella wove their fingers together, Iella's head resting against Nootau's shoulder as they waited.

Before long, Acaraho stood at the front with the Leader's Staff in his hand and addressed the crowd. He was once again wearing the loincloth and torso wrap he had adopted in support of Khon'Tor.

"Welcome. We are pleased to have you with us. As you know by now, Khon'Tor has left the leadership of the High Rocks, and it has been passed to me. My mate, the Healer, Adia, and I hope you enjoy your visit here and celebrate with us the pairings of these young males and females as they start their journeys together." He handed the meeting over to the new Overseer to conduct the ceremonies.

After quite a few pairings from the other communities, it was time for Nimida and Tar to come forward, and they quickly moved to the front to stand before Urilla Wuti.

She joined their hands together and raised them high as she pronounced Ashwea Awhidi. Tar leaned over and hugged Nimida before they stepped down together.

"Nootau'Tor and Iella Onida, please come forward."

Nootau led Iella to the front. Urilla Wuti looked

at them both with such love that Iella could have cried.

The Overseer gently took their hands and joined them together. Then, as she had done with those before, she lifted their hands high into the air and pronounced Ashwea Awhidi.

In the audience, Adia leaned into her mate, and he put his arm around her shoulder and pulled her close. He could feel her tears wetting his chest despite his leather coverings. He smiled down at her and said, "You have always deeply loved your offspring, near or far. Through the years, I watched you pray over them, worry about them. You guided them as best as you could. And because of your faithfulness and steadfastness, they have grown to find love that will walk with them the rest of their journey home."

Adia tucked her face back into Acaraho's chest and wrapped her arms around him as tight as she could.

To the side, Nadiwani stood holding An'Kru as she watched both of Adia's offspring be paired with their true loves. Unbeknownst to her, the High Protector, Awan, was watching her. An'Kru cooed and stuck his little hand out as if pointing somewhere. Nadiwani followed the gesture, only to see Awan's eyes on her. She blushed and went back to tending her charge.

That night, Nimida and Tar, Nootau and Iella,

consummated their love for each other and began their journeys into the rest of their lives.

It felt to Oh'Dar as if he had been riding forever. Despite frequent stops to rest, feed, and water Storm, and for a spell, to remove the hated Waschini boots, he was for the first time ever weary of the journey. Other times, he had enjoyed the quiet. Time for reflection, planning, gratitude. But this time, he felt nervous and could not find the peace he sought.

He passed the town of Wilde Edge, outside of which Nora and her family resided. He thought of stopping but felt the need to push on to Shadow Ridge. Fall was nearly over, though for now, he was grateful for the cooler traveling temperatures.

Before long, the familiar mountainous terrain gave way to flatter expanses, and Oh'Dar knew he was nearing his destination. He knew his grandmother and Ben had no way of knowing he was coming, and the closer he got, the higher his anxiety rose.

Then he realized what it was; he was anxious about what was about to happen. In his heart, he knew he had come to a crossroads and could not turn away. But for some reason, he had a sense of dread, unusual for him, about what was to take place.

As he headed Storm down the long road that led

to the house, he looked around as if seeing it for the first time—the rolling hillside, the beautiful pines, the deciduous trees now nearly bare of their leaves, and the vast white two-story house with the long set of steps leading up to the front door. He looked across at the outbuildings—the stables, barns, and ranch hands' quarters. *Is this the last time I will see Shadow Ridge?* Oh'Dar's stomach twisted with nerves.

Soon, familiar faces came out to greet him. Mrs. Thomas, with the usual towel in her hands, dusting flour from her arms. Mac, her son, came running out of the stables, followed closely by Ben. His grandmother, Miss Vivian, waved furiously from the swing near the top of the stairs, standing up as she tried to catch his attention.

She started down the steps, and Oh'Dar's heart lurched as he saw her foot catch on the porch rug. She began to pitch forward but righted herself at the last minute.

Oh'Dar's blood ran cold. *Grandmother almost fell down the steps. She could have been killed in front of my eyes.*

He dug his heels into Storm and drove the stallion furiously, quickly closing the distance to the house. He practically flung himself off the horse and raced up the steps as fast as he could. Within seconds, his grandmother was in his arms.

"You almost fell!" he cried out. "Are you alright?"

"I'm fine, Grayson. It was nothing, really."

Oh'Dar hugged her again, burying his face in the

billowing mass of her soft auburn hair. By then, Ben had reached them both. He touched his wife on the arm, and she looked up from Oh'Dar's embrace and nodded that she was alright.

Whatever doubts Oh'Dar had about asking them to come and live with him at Kthama suddenly vanished. He knew he couldn't bear to worry about them any longer and would do all he fairly could to convince them to return with him to his world.

Surrounded by friends and family, Oh'Dar was welcomed into the warm comfortable house while one of the farmhands unfastened his bags and led Storm to the stables. Within moments, another came up the steps bringing Oh'Dar's travel bags with him and handed them inside to Mrs. Thomas.

Miss Vivian looked Oh'Dar up and down. Something had changed. What was it?

"Grayson, I cannot believe you've come home right now. What perfect timing," she said as she led him into the parlor.

Oh'Dar entered the room to see Miss Blain sitting on one of the settees, a delicate teacup in her hand. She put it down on the table beside her, draped her napkin over the arm of the chair, and rose to greet him.

She smiled as she approached. "Master Grayson. It's good to see you again."

Miss Vivian smiled profusely. "Sit down, you two. Relax while we prepare your room, Grayson. Miss Blain has come to stay for a few days; you can get to know each other again," she said.

Miss Vivian looked at Miss Blain, trying to see her through her grandson's eyes. Her beautiful thick hair was done up very becomingly. No longer confined to wearing the bulky clothing she'd switched to after Grayson developed a crush on her, she wore a satin dress that very nicely followed her curves. There was no mistaking she was still a breathtakingly beautiful woman. Miss Vivian caught herself wondering if their children would have Grayson's blue eyes, but then she doubted it since Miss Blain's were brown.

Ben was about to come into the room but thought better of it. Miss Vivian followed him, leaving her grandson and Miss Blain alone.

"What is it, dear?" she asked.

"I was going to speak with Grayson, but I can see he's already occupied."

Miss Vivian smiled conspiratorially at her husband, then glanced back into the room at the couple.

"Oh, wouldn't it be wonderful, Ben?"

"Now, Vivian," he smiled, "I hope you don't get your hopes dashed."

"But just look at them. They're perfect together."

Ben put an arm around his wife. "I'm going back to the stables. We have a lot of work to do before winter. You all enjoy some time together and I'll be back later, worn out, no doubt. Honestly, I don't know what I'd do without Mac. He's become my right-hand man. I swear he could run this place without me."

"Shhh, don't say that. You sound as if you're ready to retire!" Miss Vivian said.

"Don't worry; it'll be a long time before that happens."

◯

At dinner, Miss Vivian purposefully sat Oh'Dar right across from Miss Blain. There was no mistaking the young woman's beauty and poise, and he imagined she was exactly the kind of wife his grandmother wanted for him. And now he had to tell her that he was already bonded. Paired. Married.

And before too long. Oh'Dar pushed the food around on his plate.

"What is wrong, Master Grayson?" asked Mrs. Thomas as she brought in another bowl of freshly baked rolls.

"Everything is delicious," he answered. "Don't mind me; I just have a lot on my mind."

Out of the corner of his eye, he could see his grandmother glance at Ben. *Oh no. She thinks I mean Miss Blain. The sooner I tell her, the better, lest this become even more awkward later.*

When they'd finished eating, Miss Vivian

suggested that Oh'Dar take Miss Blain to the sitting room where a warm fire was blazing and sit a spell. Soon after they were seated, Mrs. Thomas brought them each a cup of tea, fragrant with chamomile.

Oh'Dar remembered the room, seldom used, and he also remembered that there'd been more seating before. He wondered when his grandmother or Mrs. Thomas had managed to remove enough seating that he had no option but to sit next to Miss Blain. Close. Very close together, their knees almost touching.

"What have you been doing with yourself, Master Grayson?" Miss Blain asked, taking a sip of tea. "Have you finished your studies?"

*She does not know how long I've been gone. Apparently, Grandmother hasn't had time to fill her in.* "I'm not finished with my studies. But I don't think I'll continue." He took a deep breath. "Miss Blain, I don't mean to be so forward as to believe it matters to you, but I feel I need to tell you that I'm now married."

"Oh. Of course. Well, congratulations, Master Grayson," she said with an over-bright smile, looking around the room uncomfortably. "If you'll excuse me, I'm tired, and I think I'll retire for the night."

"I understand," said Oh'Dar, and setting his cup down, he stood as she rose and left the room.

Then he went looking for his grandmother. He found her coming out of the kitchen where she'd been speaking with Mrs. Thomas about the next day's meal.

"Grandmother, I need to speak with you and Ben," he said.

She looked puzzled but said nothing as she waited for Mrs. Thomas to send for Ben, who'd already gone upstairs.

Soon the three of them were in the parlor.

"Where's Miss Blain?" asked Miss Vivian. "Surely you aren't done talking already? I'd have thought you had a great deal to catch up on."

"She said she wished to retire early. That's just it, Grandmother. There's nothing for us to catch up on; there's no point in it, though I appreciate what you're trying to do."

"Told you," Ben chided his wife good-naturedly. "I said he'd see through you."

Miss Vivian looked up at the ceiling and sighed. "I just don't want you to be alone, Grayson. Ben and I are getting older. We aren't always going to be here, you know."

"Stop it, please. I can't bear the thought of you not being around. There's something I want to tell you, though it isn't how I'd expected to break the news. I've gotten married."

"Married?" His grandmother sat up straighter. "For heaven's sake, to whom?"

"To a wonderful young woman I've known all my life. We grew up as friends. Then later, everything changed, and we realized we were in love."

Vivian looked at Ben.

"Is it the one who was pregnant, to whom you returned before?" she dared to ask.

"No. That was just a friend. A dear friend, but just a friend."

"Why didn't you bring her here for us to meet her?"

"I didn't think it wise."

"Oh," she said.

Silence.

"Grayson," Ben asked in the gap. "Is she one of the locals? One of the people you were raised with?"

"Something like that," he answered. "But I feel terrible; when I told Miss Blain—that's when she went upstairs."

"Don't feel too bad. When you came home at what seemed to be just the right time, I got my hopes up because Miss Blain was already here. I only want you to be happy, Grayson," his grandmother said.

"I am happy, Grandmother. Except for so often having to be away from you both."

"Well," said Ben, slapping his knees and rising to his feet. "It's very late, and I can see that you're exhausted. Tomorrow is a new day. What say we sleep on everything and get a fresh start in the morning? You can tell us all about your new bride then; I know your grandmother will be dying to hear everything."

After discussing the news with Mrs. Thomas, Miss Vivian retired for the night. Up in the bedroom, she let out a long sigh from her side of the bed.

Ben looked at her, then took off his reading glasses and placed them and his book on the bed table. "I know you're disappointed," he said.

She moved closer to him and cuddled up, resting her head on his chest. He stroked her beautiful auburn hair.

"What are we to do? If he's married one of the locals from back wherever he was raised, his life is now even more tied to there. Wherever *there* is. And if he does not want to bring her here, we'll see him less and less. And we'll never see our grandchildren."

Ben rubbed her back gently as she continued to rest against him.

"I don't know, dear. I don't have the answer. But perhaps when we spend more time with Oh'Dar, it won't be as gloomy as it sounds at the moment. Perhaps he didn't mean he'd *never* bring her.

"Now, let's get some rest. Things always look worse when one's tired," he added, and he reached over just far enough to turn down the gas lamp, letting the comfort of darkness fill the room.

☾

When Oh'Dar came downstairs the next morning, Mrs. Thomas congratulated him on his marriage. "You *have* taken us by surprise." Then she told him that his grandmother and Ben were out seeing Miss Blain off. She'd risen early and asked for someone to drive her into town.

"Leaving so soon?" he asked, though in his heart he was not surprised.

"She said she wanted to get an early start home," Mrs. Thomas explained.

"I understand. For what it's worth, I'm sorry I spoiled Grandmother's dream," he sighed.

"Your grandmother only wants you to be happy. Whatever that looks like. They're getting on in years, Master Grayson. They understand they won't live forever, and they don't want you to be alone. Miss Vivian's dream has always been that you'd live here and take over Shadow Ridge. When you said you weren't sure that it was wise to bring your wife here, the future she's pictured pretty much vanished."

Oh'Dar seated himself, and Mrs. Thomas brought over a large plate of biscuits and a thick slab of freshly churned butter.

"You know, from the moment you first set foot here, and after the shock of your being alive wore off, her first thought was that you'd fill Shadow Ridge with grandchildren," she smiled.

Oh'Dar looked up at her and smiled back a bit sadly. *Great Spirit, give me the words to say. But whatever is meant to be, help me surrender to your will.*

Miss Vivian and Ben came in.

"We've just said our goodbyes to Miss Blain," said Ben, pulling out a chair for his wife before sitting down himself. "She asked us to give you her congratulations again." He took the large bowl of scrambled eggs in front of him and offered to dish some up for the others. "This looks delicious. Good thing someone gets up early," he said, winking at Mrs. Thomas, who was just leaving the dining room.

"I need to talk to you both," Oh'Dar sighed, "after we've eaten."

"Oh, no. Please, Grayson. Please don't tell me you're leaving Shadow Ridge never to return."

'No, Grandmother. It isn't that. But you're right that I'm feeling the strain of having to live in three places," he exclaimed. "Dividing up my life, and wherever I am, always feeling that I should be somewhere else."

"Three places, Grayson?" Ben looked at Miss Vivian and frowned. 'You mean two. Here and wherever you were raised, don't you?" he asked.

"Please, when we're done, I'll do my best to explain to you as much as I dare. At least, as well as I can."

They ate the rest of their meal in silence. Oh'Dar made sure to take his time savoring the warm biscuits and the rich creamy butter. *I know that in the big picture, it's trivial, but I should miss these so much if I knew I'd never eat them again*, he thought as he took another bite.

With breakfast done, Oh'Dar asked them to come for a short walk with him.

"Not far; I just don't want to be overheard," he explained.

"Let's go to your grandmother's favorite garden. Even though most of the blooms are faded, it's still a beautiful and private spot."

It was a truly serene location, with flowering vines covering the trellises that made an enclosure, in the middle of which were several wooden seats.

When they were comfortable, Oh'Dar found he was so nervous that he had to stand up again.

"I've never told you about my past because I could never find a way. Partly out of the need to protect those who raised me, partly out of a fear that you couldn't possibly understand the world I grew up in. Now I know you think I was raised by one of the local tribes, and in part, that's true. And it is as you thought; I've married a woman from the tribe that helped raise me. Her name is Acise, and she's the daughter of the Chief."

Vivian looked at Ben, who nodded toward Grayson as if saying to let him continue.

"If you were to meet her, you'd understand why there could never be any other for me but her. She's kind and gracious and smart. And yes, beautiful. I'm excited about the life that lies ahead for us. But I'm also torn because I long to be here with you. Each time I leave Shadow Ridge, it tears my heart out. I worry that I'll never see you again. Each time I return, I fear I'll find out that I've lost one or both of you. I'm miserable, and the only solution I can come up with seems impossible and too much to ask."

"What are you trying to say, Grayson? Please, just speak frankly," Ben encouraged him.

"I can't keep living like this, going from one place to the other. Always feeling torn, always being worried. Yet I can't bear the long periods between seeing you—and them—again. I wish you could all be in the same place."

Ben frowned. "Are you asking us to come live with you, in your—I'm sorry I don't know what to call it."

"Village. It's called the village. Its people are called the Brothers."

Ben shifted in his seat and looked at his wife.

Oh'Dar looked away and said a silent prayer.

"Why don't you tell us what living there is like," Ben encouraged him.

"It's set in beautiful surroundings. There's a river nearby that brings resources and bounty. The game is plentiful, and throughout the warm seasons, there are berries and nuts for easy harvest. The children fill the village with joy and laughter. Family fires dot the night landscape, and loved ones sit together reminiscing about the past day or planning the next – just as we do here. They're deeply spiritual, giving praise and thanks to the Great Spirit which provides for all their needs."

"It sounds beautiful," his grandmother said.

"It is. And there's much love and goodwill among the people there. But it's nothing like your life here. It's primitive. Until I came here, I didn't realize just how different my life has been from how you live. There are no conveniences; everything is earned from the land—clothing, tools, bedding, shelter. What they don't produce themselves or don't make with their own hands does not exist. I know I'm not telling you much that's new, but I must spell it out."

Vivian looked over at Ben, her face expressionless.

Oh'Dar continued. "There's laughter and celebration and joy. But there's also heartbreak and sorrow. Life is the same as here, only harder. Couples marry, have children, say goodbye to their loved ones, and lean on their faith to help them through. We sleep on mats filled with grasses and moss. We wake at first light, we retire at nightfall when we can no longer keep our eyes open."

Oh'Dar stopped; everything he had told them was true, but he was leaving out the most important parts.

Overcome, he sat down and rested his face in his hands. "I can't do this," he said to no one. "I can't."

"What can't you do?" his grandmother asked, getting up and coming to sit beside him.

"I can't ask you to give up your life here. Everything you know. Everything you've built. To leave all this and come and live an entirely different existence." He raised his head to look at her, "I know what it's like to be an Outsider. It's painful. Hard. Lonely. You question everything. Why you're there, whether you're making the right choices, if you'll ever feel that you fit in. I can't ask you to give up the familiarity and ease of what you have here to live such an uncomfortable life as I've had to, never feeling that you truly belong."

His grandmother put her arm around him and pulled him down to rest his head on her shoulder.

"It's alright, Grayson. We love you, and we understand. We only want to be with you and share what is left of our lives with you. You've suffered enough. If what you need is for us to come back and live in your world with you, I'm willing to try. To see how it would be to do so." She looked over at Ben as she spoke, seeing him nod his agreement.

Embarrassed, Oh'Dar stifled a sob and lifted his head. He squeezed his eyes with his fingers.

"It's worse than that, Grandmother. There's no *try*. If you come to live with us, it's a one-way journey. Once there, once you join us, you can never return to the White world."

"Why not?" she asked. "Mrs. Thomas and Mac and the farmhands can keep everything running here. We don't need to amass any more wealth; we have more than enough to last our lifetimes and yours. And probably your grandchildren's as well. And when we pass, Shadow Ridge and everything else we have will come to you."

Oh'Dar extracted himself from his grandmother's embrace and stood up.

"It's impossible. No matter how I try to explain, you'll never be able to believe it." No longer able to contain his grief, even though he was a grown man, tears rolled down his face. He impatiently dashed them away with his arm.

His grandmother rose and took his other hand in hers. "Grayson, I can't bear to see you like this. You say it's impossible to make us understand. I don't think it's impossible to understand. I don't see why we can't understand what it would be like to live in a village, carry water, build fires, chop wood? It isn't so difficult to imagine, and we know of the local tribes, those you call the Brothers. There's nothing secret about them. Is there more you aren't telling us? Are there enemies? Is there sickness? Would our lives be somehow in danger?"

Oh'Dar shook his head. *No, no.* He swallowed hard. It was now or never.

"What if I told you that the Brothers and the White People aren't the only people on the planet—" The word didn't easily roll off his tongue. It took an effort not to say Etera.

"Well, we know they're not. There are other groups of people certainly. Different skin colors and different hair colors. Why, look at my hair, it's very obviously not the color of yours or your father's. Even your older brother, Louis—his hair was always an unnatural shade of bright orange. I know he always hated it." She winced as the name brought up painful memories she'd tried to bury.

"No, I know that. I know that there are different hair colors. Different skin tones. I'm talking more different than that."

"Different how?" she asked.

"Different different. Different enough that they have to keep their existence hidden from the rest of Et— The world. They're so different that some people would try to harm them because they're frightening if you don't know them. But there's no need to be afraid; they're good, kind people. They're deeply respectful of the planet and every living thing on it. They're peace-loving, and they care for the weak and the helpless. They worship the same creator you do, though by a different name. They mean no one harm—I'm proof of that."

Oh'Dar stopped so his words could settle in them.

"The female who found me, rescued me, and took me back to where she lived was their Healer. She was the one who came upon me, somehow overlooked during my parents' massacre. She raised me, cared for me. She taught me the ways of her people. Later, her husband took me under his wing and mentored me. Taught me how to hunt, forage, protect myself. Taught me to read the night skies, taught me the names and calls of the birds. How to pick fruit only when the vine is ready to release it. To take only as much as we need and share it with others. Laughter, tears, joy—all of what you know of life is the same for them. Only, because they're different, they must keep themselves separate and live in hiding."

Oh'Dar paused long enough for his grandmother to ask, "And these are the people who raised you? But they aren't from the local village you spoke of earlier?"

"Yes, those are the ones who raised me. When I was older, I was also helped by a man who is now the Brothers' Chief. He taught me to ride, shoot with a bow and arrow, skin animals, and prepare hides. His wife's father was a White Man, and she taught me to speak English. But she also taught me to sew and to weave, and to plant healing herbs and flowers. Between her and my mother, I gained extensive knowledge of natural medicine. How to treat a fever, an infection, even how to set a broken bone."

"So, those two women, they were like, medicine women?"

"Yes. Healers. Healers to each of their people."

"No wonder you wanted to be a doctor," Ben said quietly.

"What I am, what I've become, everything you know me to be, every bit of whatever good I have within me, is a product of the combined love and guidance and protection I received under their care. My mother, Adia, suffered greatly for her decision to rescue me. But she never regretted it. She could have walked away and left me there to die a terrible death, knowing that before long, the predators would find me. No one would have known had she taken the easier route. But instead, she saved me, brought me back to her community, breaking Sacred Law to do so, and raised me as her own."

Oh'Dar stopped talking, and the birdsong in the background filled the silence.

"Would they accept us?" his grandmother asked.

"Yes. They would accept you; in all honesty, they agreed that I should ask you to come. You'd be welcomed. You'd be respected. Protected. Perhaps to an extent, even revered. You'd have purpose there, but in time your clothes would wear out and have to be replaced by hand-sewn skins. Your shoes would eventually also be made of animal skins. There'd be no biscuits and gravy. No butter. No soft, cool sheets to slip between on a hot summer night. No fine dishes or other appointments. No oil lamps to break the darkness. You'd be leaving behind everything you know. Forever."

Oh'Dar searched his grandparents' faces as they looked up at him. He felt a sense of peace wash over him and let his thoughts rest. *There. I've done my best. Now the path must unfold as it will.*

"Don't give me an answer one way or the other yet," he said. Please sit with what I've told you. Pray about it. No matter what you decide, it'll be the right decision. And if you decide against it, I'll still return to Shadow Ridge as often as I can. Because you're my family, and I'll love you and need you forever and always."

Miss Vivian let go of the tears she'd been keeping back. They dropped into the soft handkerchief she was holding, and she brought it up to her eyes.

Ben looked at the young man he'd come to think of as a son, and though he'd had no part in the young man's upbringing, felt enormous pride in the caliber of the person who stood before him.

Oh'Dar hugged and kissed his grandmother and then hugged Ben. Then he silently turned and walked off toward the stables to check on Storm.

Vivian looked at her husband. "What do you think?" Ben shook his head. "We must consider this carefully, Vivian. Whatever we decide, I have the feeling we're being faced with a once-in-a-lifetime decision, a fork in the path that won't come again."

Vivian nodded and dabbed her eyes further with her handkerchief. Eventually, they rose and went about their business and didn't speak of it between themselves for some time.

Oh'Dar filled the following days helping Ben in the stables and working with the ranch hands, mending fences, and doing other chores. In between, despite her protests that this was not man's work, he helped Mrs. Thomas do laundry, change bedding, even bake. If by some miracle they decided to go with him and this was his last visit to Shadow Ridge, he wanted to experience as much of the life as possible. His favorite was kneading bread, the soft squishy warm consistency that gave way under his hands.

"Are you enjoying your visit home?" she asked, making light conversation.

"I always enjoy being home, and I especially enjoy it when you bake bread," he grinned.

"I appreciate your help. Especially taking it out of the hot oven. I can hardly keep up with your appetite for it, though," Mrs. Thomas chided him gently.

Oh'Dar rubbed his face, leaving a dusting of flour on his nose. Mrs. Thomas laughed and reached out with the hem of her apron to clean it off.

"Can I fill the pot for you and set it on the cookstove?" he asked, knowing that the large iron pot was heavy for her.

"That would be very kind of you," and she nodded to where it hung overhead. "Once all the bread has finished rising, you can help me load it into the oven if you would."

Oh'Dar lifted down the heavy pot, took it to the sink, and grasped the hand pump to fill it with water. Once filled, he carried it over and set it down on the cookstove. Then he reached up into the cupboard, took the lid down, and put it on top. Everywhere he looked, there was something he could not imagine his grandparents living without. Iron pots, cookstoves, indoor water. Chairs, sofas, mattresses. Lacy curtains billowing in the breeze. The chime of the clock on the quarter-hour, gently echoing upstairs from the dining room below. The list went on and on. He let out a heavy sigh.

Slowly over the following days, he resigned himself to accepting that they wouldn't be coming back with him. But he'd done what he came to do and would live with and make the best of whatever happened.

## CHAPTER 10

As time passed, life had returned to normal at the Brothers' village, with the glaring exception of what to do about Pajackok's crimes. To Honovi and Acise's surprise, Snana had not gotten over what they believed to be her infatuation with Pajackok. Instead, she spent every moment she could with him, even begging her parents to let her move into his family shelter.

"Are you saying you wish to be bonded? That you would take Pajackok as your life-walker?" her mother asked her, brow creased with disbelief.

"I know you do not believe that we are truly in love, but we are."

"That is what *you* say, but what of Pajackok?" Is'Taqa hated to ask but had to. He finally had his anger at Pajackok's behavior under control.

"He would say yes if I asked him," she said,

lowering her eyes. Then she looked up and said, "Do I have your blessing to ask him?"

Honovi sighed and glanced at Is'Taqa.

"Is this what you really want? Are you prepared for others to believe he only chose you because he could not have your sister?"

"I have worried about that, but now I know he truly loves me for being me. And that Acise no longer lives in his heart." She looked over at her sister as she spoke.

"I believe that Snana is right," said Acise. "I see how he looks at her, how his eyes follow her as she moves about. Regardless of whatever feelings he said he had, he was never devoted to me like that. Sometimes I wonder if he thought we belonged together simply because there seemed a natural momentum to it. For whatever reason, people just assumed we would end up together. I think that belief may somehow have taken on a life of its own."

She cleared her throat. "And in all fairness, I only chose Pajackok because I was trying to get over Oh'Dar. When he left, I was crushed, and to ease my pain, I wanted someone to want me; I wanted a future to look forward to. I did not choose Pajackok because he was the one I wanted; I chose him because I felt I had lost forever the one I did want. I made it worse by telling Pajackok we could be bonded. If I had been honest with myself and him, it would never have escalated as it did."

Chief Is'Taqa sat quietly, taking in the words of

his life-walker and his daughters. *The wise man listens carefully to the words of others, not only with his ears but with his heart and his soul.* These were words Chief Ogima Adoeete had taught him. *The anger I feel toward Pajackok is natural, but it isn't the only way of looking at the situation.*

"I just want Snana to find the happiness I have with Oh'Dar," Acise added.

"The cold weather is almost set in," said Honovi, looking at her silent mate.

"What?" asked Acise? "What does that mean?"

"Your sister has said she wants to return with Pajackok and live in the shelter he built," said Honovi. "If they're going to live there, they will need to leave very soon."

"And your father has not decided whether they will be allowed to do that. Or, at least whether Snana will be allowed to go with him," she added, looking pointedly at Is'Taqa.

"Not allowed?" Snana cried out. "What, as some type of punishment for what Pajackok did?"

Her father finally spoke. "I have not decided what, if anything, to do about Pajackok kidnapping you. Ordinarily, there should be serious consequences.

"As far as his leaving is concerned, you're just headstrong enough that if he were to leave without you, which I do not believe he would, I can imagine you might go after him even if I ordered you not to. Perhaps with disastrous results."

"If he is willing to leave his family and his life here, what more consequences could there be?" Acise asked.

"The fact of what Pajackok did cannot be ignored. Whether or not I, as Chief, determine a penalty for his actions, a penalty is still required. And he is the only one who can free himself of that."

Pajackok knew everyone was still talking about him, the fights with Oh'Dar, his kidnapping of Snana. He had shamed his family and himself. And like it or not, he knew that by his association with Snana, he was also shaming her. After much thought, and having made up his mind about the right thing to do, Pajackok began preparing to leave the village and his family, and the woman he loved.

"What are you doing? It looks like you are getting ready to leave," Snana said to him.

"It would be best to travel before the hard weather sets in," he said.

"I will have my things ready. I only have a few belongings I wish to take back with me."

He stopped and turned to her, "You must stay here."

"What are you saying? You do not want me to come back with you?"

The look in her eyes crushed him. "I think it best that you stay here with your family. I was wrong to take you away. And there is nothing I can do to make that right."

"But I love you. And you love me—I know you do. I do not understand why you are talking like this. You promised you would not leave without me."

Pajackok looked off into the far distance, searching for words.

"I have dishonored myself, and I do not wish also to dishonor you by association. You would have a better life here with another brave."

"I do not want another brave. I want you." She was practically in tears.

"And I want you. But it is unfair to take you away from everyone else you love and let them be forever displeased with you. And I cannot stay here any longer," Pajackok said, knowing his resolve would die if he did not soon create distance between Snana and himself.

"Bond with me," she said.

"What?"

"Bond with me. I choose you. I choose you as my life-walker."

Pajackok stopped, knowing the next words he said could never be taken back. One way or the other.

He looked down at her, at her beautiful dark eyes, her soft cheeks, the long gleaming hair which fell all the way down her back. He thought of her wit, the way her temper would flare, and how, no matter what, she would stand up to him. Their time together, the teasing, the laughter. Holding her in his arms in the dark. Sitting by the fire and cracking nuts to eat while twilight descended. He remembered how she had done everything she could to keep her heart from him and how he had done everything he could to break that resolve. He knew he would never love another. Had never loved another, despite what he had thought and said before. And at that moment, he knew what he had to do.

"Come with me," Pajackok said. He left what he was doing and led Snana into the center of the village.

"Everyone, come, please," he shouted and then shouted it again. Slowly the rest of the village started to assemble. Someone ran to get Snana's family.

Pajackok waited until everyone was there, looking at him and waiting for him to speak. His father and mother stood side by side, their hands joined.

"Hear me out, please," he said. "It is no secret that I have shamed myself and my family. I have acted imprudently. I did what I thought I had to do, fighting Oh'Dar of the People for the woman I thought I belonged with. Then, when our intended bonding was set aside, and Acise chose Oh'Dar, I left in anger and later returned and abducted her sister, Snana, who stands here with me. You all know the story. I am not reminding you as much as I am declaring the truth."

He looked around the circle at everyone staring at him, all unmoving.

"There is no excuse for how I behaved, so I will offer none. I am prepared to leave, this time forever."

He walked over to stand before Chief Is'Taqa. "For what I have done, there can be no forgiveness. So I stand here not asking for it, but only to admit to my crimes and failings and to take responsibility for my actions. When I took your daughter, I did so out of loneliness and a wish for companionship. But also for revenge. Yes, I freely admit to that. But wisdom has softened my heart and opened my eyes. What started out as revenge changed, and I came to love Snana. To truly, deeply love her. The idea of being without her is more than I can bear. I did not set out to fall in love with her, but I have, and for me, there will be no escape from that truth, just as there can be no forgiveness for what I have done.

"If you wish to punish me for my actions, that is your right," he said to the Chief. "And I accept whatever you decree. Only, please know I love your daughter in a way I could not have thought possible, and if I could undo the harm I have done, and the anguish I have caused, I would."

When the Chief did not speak, Pajackok turned to Acise. "I am sorry for the trouble I caused you. I was embarrassed and angry when you chose Oh'Dar over me. My pride was hurt, as well as my sense of entitlement to you as your promised life-walker. Now, I am grateful that it worked out as it did. I truly believe that you belong with Oh'Dar, just as I believe that I belong with Snana."

"I hold no ill will toward you, Pajackok," answered Acise. "And neither does Oh'Dar. I wish you only happiness. And I wish the same for my sister." She looked over at Snana, who was standing stiffly just inside the circle of onlookers.

Chief Is'Taqa kept his silence, knowing there was more that must be said.

Snana shook off her paralysis and walked over to him. "Papa. I know what Pajackok did was wrong, and so does he. When he took me away, I was scared and angry. All I could think of was getting back home. I was worried sick over what you and everyone else must be going through. I wanted so much to let you know I was alright, but I could not. In time, I realized I had either to find a routine or lose my mind. I busied myself with all the things you taught me to do, Papa. I honed stones for weapons, I tanned hides. And I gathered herbs, roots, flowers, and leaves for medicines as you taught me, Momma. I tried to keep my mind occupied as I waited for a plan to reveal itself.

"During all that time, Pajackok was nothing but kind to me. He brought me small treasures—flowers, colored stones. In a hundred ways, he showed me kindness after kindness. Whatever anger he felt about what happened here before, he never once took it out on me. During that time, my heart finally softened, and I saw him for his true self. Who knows, if hurt enough, what any of us is capable of? We make mistakes. We learn. Hopefully, we grow. And when we accept our wrongdoing, we try to make amends. And we pray that others will allow us to live down the wrongs we have done, and despite our failings, to find whatever joy we can."

She turned to Pajackok. "I love you. I love you, and I want never to be apart from you. My home and my family are here. But my heart is wherever you are. Pajackok, I choose you as my life-walker. Now and forever," and she reached out her hands to his.

Pajackok looked into her eyes and then took her hands.

Chief Is'Taqa nodded. The last piece had fallen into place. Then he spoke. "It is as you have said."

All eyes immediately turned to him.

"Pajackok, it is as you have rightly said. There is nothing that can change what you have done. But in the wisdom and grace of the Great Spirit, even our failings can be turned to good. Out of every difficulty, every challenge, even in the darkest hour, when it seems all has been lost, let us never forget that guiding everything is the hand of the all-wise and loving Great Spirit who sees our mistakes even before we make them. Who then moves ahead of us and opens a new path on which we are further blessed if we have realized the error of our ways."

He grasped the joined hands of his daughter and Pajackok. "Together, you must now choose your life's direction. You must decide whether you will stay and build your life here or return to the place where your love first blossomed and continue your journey from there."

He paused a moment, honoring the sacred mood that had descended on those present. "Know that whatever you decide, your choice will be the right one. The choice that will lead you to what awaits on your walk together through this lifetime."

Pajackok looked at Snana. Her brown eyes lifted to his as she eagerly waited for him to speak.

"I will be your life-walker," he said.

Snana fell into his arms, resting her head on his chest. Then she turned to her mother. "Momma, I wish for us to be bonded as soon as possible."

"We will make the arrangements," Honovi replied warmly. "We should be ready in a few days."

Snana broke into a huge smile.

Honovi looked at her partner. "You are a wise Chief," she said. "And a wise father."

"Wisdom is carried in on the wings of patience," was his reply, though his eyes sparkled at her.

○

The days passed quickly, and soon it was time for the bonding ceremony. Snana had asked if she could wear the ornate buckskin Acise had worn when she and Oh'Dar were bonded. Acise was honored and delighted to help Snana prepare. When everything was ready, the village came together for the ritual.

After a period of drumming and chanting, Chief Is'Taqa raised his staff, and the drums silenced. As he wove it through the air, he announced, "Today we celebrate not only the return of two of our children but also their bonding as life-walkers. I ask the Great Spirit for blessings on my youngest daughter, Snana, and the brave, Pajackok, son of Tac'agawa."

Chief Is'Taqa took their hands and joined them together and raised them. On cue, the drumming and chanting started up again and fell silent. Then, after each statement, a short burst of drumming broke out, "May your love last all of your days. May you grow wise together. May you be blessed with many children."

The Chief lowered his staff, and the drumming rose in fervor, signaling that Snana and Pajackok were now bonded as one.

A spirit of gaiety filled everyone, and there was much dancing and laughing.

As the morning progressed, Honovi asked her daughter, "Are you sure you do not wish to use our shelter for your first joining?"

"No, thank you. We still want to leave for the home Pajackok made. It will take a couple of days to get there, but we can wait."

Her mother said nothing, understanding the importance of their first bonded coupling.

After the celebration had wound down, Pajackok and Snana said their goodbyes. At the Chief's direction, one of the braves had earlier prepared Snana's favorite horse, Nawaba, for her to ride.

"Do you really mean to return to us?" Honovi was afraid to ask but could not help herself.

"Yes, we will be back very soon. This is not good-bye, Momma, I promised."

Fighting tears, Honovi nodded in great relief.

"We just want some time together, and we want to gather some items to bring back. Then we will return to build our own shelter before the cold weather sets in."

Pajackok spoke for a few moments with his parents and brothers and then turned back to Snana. "Are you ready?"

Once both were mounted, Snana again promised her parents, "We will be back before too long."

Pajackok nodded his confirmation and looked across at his life-walker.

She brought her horse close to his and leaned across to kiss him, sweetly, gently, one of so many that would fill the days and nights to come. Then she looked into his eyes.

"Let us go," she whispered. "Our new life starts today."

## CHAPTER 11

Back at Shadow Ridge, life continued as usual. Mrs. Thomas stayed busy running the household with Miss Vivian's nominal supervision. Ben looked after the business end, and he and his hands took care of the horses and the fields.

One day, while working together in the barn, Ben stopped a moment, stretched out his back with a sigh, and turned to Oh'Dar. "What is your life like there? How do you spend your time?" He shoveled another fork of hay into a stall.

"When I was growing up, there was always something to learn. Because of the size difference, I couldn't play much with the other children my age." Oh'Dar slipped a glance at Ben to see if there was any reaction to that statement. "But my brother and my father made sure I was not lonely and engaged me in activities suited to me. I learned the changing pattern of the night sky, the phases of the moon, how to plant, harvest, prepare stores for winter, and other lean times. My father taught me to spear fish, to track, to clean and preserve hides. At the Brothers' village, I learned how to make a bow and arrows and how to ride. I had a rich upbringing."

"And now that you're grown?" Ben asked.

Just then, Miss Vivian came in with two glasses of tea.

"Sit down and join us for a while," said Ben. "Grayson was just telling me what his day-to-day life is like at—at wherever he grew up."

"Kthama. It's called Kthama," said Oh'Dar. "I split my time between the Brothers' village and Kthama. At the village, I help with daily chores just as I do here. There's always something that needs to be done —carrying water, hunting, planting, harvesting, fixing and reusing items. But I have new duties now, as I'm teaching my people Whitespeak."

Neither Ben nor Vivian asked, both figuring out what the term meant.

"You have a school?" his grandmother asked.

"Yes. My people have no written language, and for various reasons, the Leader asked me to start a school," Oh'Dar explained. "I'm copying some of the techniques Miss Blain used to teach me. I think it's going well."

"So there are children there too." His grandmother's eyes lit up.

"Oh, yes. There are quite a few children of

various ages. The whole community helps raise them and look after them—though, of course, they still have their parents," he added.

"When that wolf came to Shadow Ridge," said Ben, "you called out to it in a different language. Is that the language they speak?"

"Yes. As I said, the wife of the Chief taught me to speak English, although, of course, I also grew up speaking their language."

"So we wouldn't be able to communicate except among ourselves?" his grandmother asked.

"Before, I would have said yes. But as the school progresses, more and more are learning English. We also have a sign language, which is easier to learn at first, I think."

Oh'Dar saw his grandmother look over at Ben but could not read her expression.

"Where do they live, Grayson?" asked Ben.

"They live in communities. A few years back, there was a terrible sickness—the same one I had when I first lived here—and we lost a lot of our males, so now there aren't enough to go around."

"They share the men?" Miss Vivian's voice broke.

"No. No, not like that. Sorry, Grandmother. Males and females are always paired—married—but some females won't be paired because of the shortage of males. Because they're chosen for each other based on their bloodlines, the children are born healthy. Ben, you'd understand that."

"Do they live in homes like the locals—the Brothers—build?" asked Ben.

Oh'Dar swallowed hard. "In caves. They live in caves." *Well, that did it. If nothing else did, now they're sure not to come.*

"Caves," his grandmother repeated.

"Yes, caves. Well, an elaborate cave system. There are separate rooms for small meetings and a large area where people can eat together, and community meetings are held. The families have separate living and sleeping quarters, while some, usually the unpaired—unmarried—males, prefer to live together more communally."

"Well," his grandmother said. "I'd better take this glassware back up to the house before it gets broken." She rose and took the empty glasses from Ben and Oh'Dar. "Don't be late for dinner. I think Mrs. Thomas has something special prepared for tonight," she said before she left.

"Caves, son?" said Ben when they were alone.

"I know. But what can I say; it's the truth. I know it's too much to ask of you."

"We haven't decided against it. We just need to learn more."

"I can only tell you so much, Ben. I've probably shared too much as it is. And it only goes so far, anyway. The reality would be better and also harder than I can do justice to with words."

"Let's finish here and get cleaned up. This old back could use a rest, that's for sure," said Ben.

In his room, Oh'Dar lay on his back on the soft Waschini mattress, waiting to be called down for dinner. *The leaves are off the trees, and the temperatures have dropped. I must head back in the next few days. There's no way to make my grandparents understand what they'd be getting into, and I must let it go. I haven't even tried to tell them about the Sarnonn. It would be a huge mistake to let them come, only for them to find they'd made a terrible mistake when they inevitably meet Haan and his people. Then what? Oh, Great Spirit, how do I even start to tell them about the Sarnonn?*

They'd just sat down to dinner, and the sound of the clock was still echoing in the background. Oh'Dar had come to love it, the melodic tones that marked the day's passing.

Mrs. Thomas had just started setting the different dishes and bowls on the table when there was a knock at the front door.

She came back shortly and said, "Neighbor Mason is here. He's asking for you, Ben."

Ben and Jacob Mason had been friends for a long time, as had Jacob's wife and Miss Vivian. The Morgan and Mason children had grown up playing with each other.

Ben tossed his napkin on his side plate and rose to go to the door. Oh'Dar followed him.

"I'm sorry to interrupt your dinner, Ben, but there's a disturbance down at my place, and I could use some help."

"What is it, Jacob?"

"Something in the woods has been bothering our horses and pigs," he replied.

"Coyotes? Bears? What is it?"

"That's just it. Sarah and the grandkids saw it moving down an old deer path, among the trees. Then last night, it was standing inside the tree line in the dark. All they could see was a partial silhouette, but they're scared to death. It never came that close to the house before. Nothing like anything we've seen recently." He hesitated. "Sarah says it's a dead ringer for the old Wood Walker that people around here talked about maybe twenty-five, thirty years ago. Do you remember that?'

Ben nodded slowly. "Yes. Yes, I do. Never caught it, though, and eventually, it just left or disappeared somehow. Scared everyone to death, if I remember, though it never did any other harm. After a while, it kinda became part of our local legend. Later, townsfolk even used to joke about it.

"Grayson, tell your grandmother I'm going to help Jacob. I'll be back as soon as I can."

"I'm going with you," said Oh'Dar. "It sounds like you need as much help as you can get."

Jacob nodded. "He's right, Ben. In fact, if you

could grab a couple of your farmhands, maybe together we could track down this new Wood Walker —if that's what it is."

"Well, let's get going. On our way, we'll stop down by the bunker and pick up Sam and Wiley," said Ben.

The three men left and collected the others. They all seized long rifles, and Ben handed one to Oh'Dar. "Here. Just in case. If it's as big as they say it is, we'll need all the firepower we can get."

Before long, they'd made it to the Mason place and were standing where Jacob's wife had said she last saw it. It was dark, and they got comfortable, preparing for a long wait.

"Shouldn't we be off looking for it?" asked one of Ben's hands.

"Years past, word was that going out to look for it never worked. Whatever it is, it seems to be a master at hiding," said Jacob.

"Why is it coming round now?" mused Wiley. "It's been something like twenty-five years since it was last seen. I wonder if it's the same creature."

Oh'Dar was listening intently, still trying to figure out what they were talking about. "Is it a big bear?" he asked.

"No, it's not a bear. At first, everyone thought it was. Strangest thing is, when it came around, there were always trees broken off partly up the trunk," Jacob explained. "I've seen some more over the past few days."

"*Trees broken?*" Oh'Dar tried to steady his voice. "What do you mean?"

"Young trees snapped in two, higher than a person could do. Nothing that would happen naturally; something has to do that on purpose. It's the darndest thing that apparently happens only when that creature comes around," Jacob explained.

Oh'Dar's heart started to pound. *It couldn't be. Could it?*

"What else, Mr. Mason?" he asked. "What else goes on when it shows up?" Oh'Dar tried to quell the urgency in his voice.

"As far as I know, it only showed up twenty-five, maybe thirty years ago. And now. So we don't know a lot. There were footprints then. Huge footprints. And this time, the tree breaks are happening again. That's pretty much it."

"You mentioned the horses and your livestock," ventured Oh'Dar.

"Whatever it is, it doesn't hurt them. Just stirs them up. Almost like it wants us to know it's here—but it never does any harm. Beats the heck out of me," Jacob said.

"What do we do if we see it? Do we shoot it?" asked Sam.

"No!" exclaimed Oh'Dar, before catching himself. "I mean, no. No. If it isn't hurting anyone, why would we want to kill it?"

Ben stared at Oh'Dar for the longest time. "Grayson's right. No need to be rash. If it's not